BEVERLY GRAY'S SURPRISE

"A rock slide!" Mr. Brewster shouted. "Get close to the wall!"

BEVERLY GRAY'S
SURPRISE

By CLAIR BLANK

CLOVER BOOKS

McLOUGHLIN BROS.
NEW YORK

Contents

BEVERLY GRAY'S SURPRISE

They crouched down together like two conspirators

CHAPTER I

Love and Mystery

THE scent of flowers filled the church as the young man and the girl before the altar pledged their love to each other forever. Then hushed attention gave way to music that burst into crescendo as the couple turned to come down the aisle.

"I say, doesn't she look lovely?" Terry Cartwright whispered to Beverly Gray.

"Beautiful!" Beverly agreed.

When she glanced up at the tall young Englishman by her side, she saw that his eyes were not on Lois, the bride, but on the maid of honor, Lenora Whitehill. Terry's affection for Lenora had never been so apparent as it was at this moment.

Lois and Jim, now Mr. and Mrs. James Stanton, moved down the aisle, and Lenora and Larry Owens, Jim's best man, fell into step behind them.

1

Sunshine streaming through the stained glass windows cast a rosy hue on the already blushing bride. Jim Stanton's handsome face showed that he was at that moment the happiest man in the world.

Larry paused to whisper in Beverly's ear:

"I wish it were us."

Beverly nodded with a smile, knowing that someday it would be.

Larry rushed away to see about the cars which were to transport the young couple and their friends to an uptown hotel for a brief reception before going to the airport.

Readers of previous BEVERLY GRAY stories are already well acquainted with the four girls who have lived together since college graduation, and also the young men who figure so importantly in their lives.

Beverly Gray, auburn-haired, ambitious reporter for the *Tribune* is engaged to Larry Owens. Shirley Parker, known to theatergoers as Dale Arden, is engaged to wealthy young Roger Garrett.

Lois Mason—Lois Stanton now—was heretofore an illustrator for *Modern Miss* magazine. The fourth in the quartette, blonde Lenora Whitehill, works as a photographer for the *Tribune*. She has yet to decide on which young man she will bestow her heart and hand.

In BEVERLY GRAY'S SCOOP, readers learned of Jim's inheritance of a fortune, the extent of which was still to be determined. Jim and Lois planned to fly to Egypt on their wedding trip to seek more information about it.

Laughter and tears of joy mingled as relatives and close friends gathered at the back of the church.

Beverly, in the midst of the throng, suddenly spied a tall, familiar figure making his way unobtrusively from the shadowy church vestibule to the door. He was stealing past the gay group, obviously intent upon escaping without being seen by anyone. Beverly decided that this would never do, and started in pursuit of him.

She stepped out into the sunshine of the church garden and looked around. The path to the gate was empty. He couldn't have gone so quickly!

"Mike!" she called. "Michael McKay, where are you?"

"Shsh!"

A black-haired young man, with sparkling dark eyes and skin tanned from the sun, stepped from behind a giant rhododendron bush and motioned to her. Hastily he looked about and drew her off the path into the seclusion of the surrounding shrubbery.

"What's the matter, Mike?" Beverly demanded. "Why are you sneaking about like this? Aren't you going to congratulate Lois and Jim?"

"I'll do that later," he said, glancing nervously over his shoulder.

"We haven't seen you in ages," Beverly continued. "You haven't been in New York all this time, have you?"

"No. I've been out in Montana—and I wish I had stayed there!" he added.

"Oh, yes," Beverly nodded. "Larry and Lenora said you were with a mining company now. What's the matter? Are you planning to surprise Lenora? Is that it?"

"I wish it were as simple as that," Mike sighed.

He motioned her to silence as someone hurried up the church path, and they crouched together like two conspirators.

"I stopped at your apartment to see Lenora, and Mrs. Callahan told me about the wedding. I thought I'd just peek in before—"

"Peek in!" Beverly echoed. "But why? We had no idea you were in town or you would have gotten a personal invitation. You know that. Why all the secrecy? One would think you were hiding from the police!"

"Exactly!" Mike said with a deep sigh. "Now you know why I don't want Lenora to see me here. That sweet, irrepressible gal might shout it to the world."

"Mike!" Beverly said in a shocked voice. "*Are* you in trouble with the police? I don't believe it!"

"I wish they didn't," he retorted with a flash of his old humor. "Haven't you, a reporter, heard that John Brewster was robbed last night? I thought it would be in headlines by this time."

"I haven't heard a thing about it," Beverly said. "Perhaps he wasn't robbed after all. Maybe you're mistaken."

"No." Mike shook his head. "I was there and I waited long enough to overhear Brewster phone the police."

"Perhaps there is something I can do to help you," Beverly said. "Tell me about it."

There was the sound of voices from the church doorway, and people began moving down the path.

"I can't explain to you now," Mike said, "but tell Lenora that no matter what she hears about me, it isn't so. I am not a thief!"

"We know that, Mike," Beverly assured him, "and we'll help you prove it. Mike, wait—"

But the young man had slipped away as Shirley Parker came down the path seeking Beverly.

"Oh, there you are, Bev!" Shirley exclaimed. "This is no time to commune with nature," she added. "It'll have to be a whirlwind reception if they're to make their plane."

"I'm coming," Beverly returned.

Mike had disappeared, but he had left her with a mystery to be solved.

CHAPTER II

An Unexpected Guest

"You practically kidnaped me!" Larry said, grinning, as he guided his car into the stream of traffic. "I'm delighted that you long to be alone with me."

Beverly laughed at his teasing.

"The others all have transportation home from the airport, and I want to talk to you."

"Did Lois's wedding help you decide on a date for ours?" he asked hopefully. "Personally, I like the way they did it—quietly, with just relatives and intimate friends. Of course," he continued, smiling at the girl beside him, "we could do it even more quietly. We could elope to Thaïland or Timbuctoo—"

"And your family would never speak to us again, nor would mine," Beverly returned promptly. "I want to talk seriously, Larry. Mike was at the wedding."

"Michael McKay?" Larry straightened. "I didn't see him. Why didn't he say hello? Has he gone snooty or something? Did you talk to him?"

"I did and he hasn't," Beverly answered the last two questions together. "Mike is in trouble, Larry."

"When hasn't Mike been in trouble?" Larry chuckled. "He was always in a jam when we were in college together. He has the knack of doing the one thing that will always get him in wrong with someone."

"This time it's with the police," Beverly said.

"Oh, come now," Larry said, smiling. "Whatever Mike has done can't be really so serious—"

"He told me so himself," Beverly replied.

She proceeded to tell Larry all about her conversation with Mike. He listened closely and when she finished he shook his head in disbelief.

"Mike's not a thief," he said. "Perhaps we can find him. If he's in town he must have gone to his apartment."

"Let's go and see," Beverly proposed. "I have the day off because of Lois's wedding—"

"But your mind is on a story," Larry teased. "I swear, Bev, you must have printer's ink in your veins."

"Every good reporter has," Beverly agreed, laughing. "Maybe Mike has given me a headline."

They drove to the house where Mike occupied a small apartment whenever he was in town. There was no answer to his bell, and they could see mail waiting in his mailbox.

Larry called the janitor and questioned him.

The small, wizened old man told them that he had had a telegram from Mike the week before, in which Mike said he would return in a day or so.

"He wanted my wife to air his apartment and get it ready for him," the janitor continued. "She always takes care of it for him. It's all ready, but he hasn't come."

"Did he send you any word as to why he was delayed?" Beverly asked.

"No, miss. But he'll be here," the old man said confidently. "Do you folks want to leave a message for him?"

"No, thanks," Larry said slowly. "We'll stop by again in a day or two."

They got back into Larry's car, and as he started the motor he asked, "Now what? We know he's in town. Why hasn't he been home?"

"If the police are looking for him they'd be sure to come here," Beverly replied. "He's afraid to go home. Is there any other place he might go?"

"The University Club!" Larry exclaimed. "Perhaps he's staying there. We'll ask, anyway."

Larry tried to locate Mike at the University Club; they spoke to people at Mike's favorite restaurants and at the gymnasium where he often went, but no one had seen him for several months.

"Who did he tell you had been robbed?" Larry inquired again.

"John Brewster," Beverly replied. "I haven't the vaguest idea who he is."

"I think he's Mike's boss," Larry told her. "Mike mentioned him in some of his letters. They were together on some sort of a mining trip out west."

"Do you suppose we could talk to Mr. Brewster?" Beverly asked. "Where's the nearest telephone?"

"There's a drugstore," Larry said, pulling into a parking space.

They went into the cool, shadowed store and consulted the telephone directory.

"There are five John Brewsters," Beverly reported, frowning. "How can we know which one we want?"

"I think the firm is called the Brewster Mining Company," Larry said. "See if that number is listed."

"Here it is." Beverly nodded. "I'll call them and ask for John Brewster."

Beverly entered the telephone booth and Larry stood in the doorway. She dialed the number, and after a moment a feminine voice answered.

"I'm sorry but Mr. Brewster is not in, and we do not expect him today," she said in answer to Beverly's query.

"Will you give me his home telephone number?" Beverly asked. "It is important that I talk with him."

"If someone else in the office can help you—?"

"Thank you, but I want to speak with Mr. Brewster."

"I am sorry, but we are not permitted to give out his home number."

There was a click and the line was silent.

"Maybe they're being swamped with questions about him," Larry said when Beverly told him what had happened.

"I'm going to call each of the five John Brewsters listed in the directory," Beverly said. "I'll find the right one!"

Larry gave her the telephone number for the first call, but the man she spoke to was not with the Brewster Mining Company. She had the same result from the next two numbers she called. The fourth John Brewster proved to be the one she wanted, but the man who answered the telephone said Mr. Brewster was not at home. He also said he could not tell her when Mr. Brewster would be home.

"At any rate, I am going to keep his address," Beverly said firmly, copying the information from the telephone directory. "I might get to talk to Mr. Brewster yet."

"It is funny," Larry mused as they went back to the car. "Most people shout the news of a robbery. I wonder if Mike was fooling you."

"I don't think so," Beverly returned. "Why should he run away from all his friends? He must be hiding from the police, and he must be afraid he might involve his friends if he went to them."

"I suppose he felt safe enough in the wedding crowd," Larry acknowledged. "It was just by chance that you saw him."

"I'm glad I did," Beverly said. "If there were only some way I could find out more about what he's supposed to have done."

"He told the right one when he told you," Larry chuckled. "You won't rest until you get to the bottom of it. Well, where to now?"

"You might as well take me home," Beverly sighed at last. "We'll have to think of something else."

"Yes," Larry agreed. He glanced at his watch. "I have to go to my office for a while; but we should celebrate your day off. Suppose Terry and I pick up you and Lenora for dinner, and then we'll go to a show."

"Fine!" Beverly exclaimed.

"It was a beautiful wedding," Lenora was sighing as, later, Beverly entered the girls' apartment. "I hope they will be very happy—but I'm lonely already."

"What? Lonely with us here?" Shirley looked up, amused. "Hi, Bev! Where did you disappear to?"

"It's a long story," Beverly replied.

"Tell us," Lenora said. "It will help to cheer me."

"It does seem strange without Lois," Shirley said. "We four have been together so long—"

"And weathered a lot of ups and downs," Lenora added, a quiver in her voice.

"Lois hasn't died, you know." Beverly laughed. "Didn't you notice how happy she was?"

" 'Happy be the bride the sun shines on!' " Lenora quoted with another sigh. "It will probably snow the day I wed."

"Are you contemplating it in the near future?" Shirley asked interestedly. "Terry follows you about like your shadow."

"I know," Lenora admitted, "but I'm just not sure yet. After all, there was Mike—" she ended dreamily.

"Have you heard from Mike?" Beverly asked quickly.

"Not in ages—drat him!" Lenora said briskly. "I believe he's forgotten how to write."

"Good old Mike," Shirley mused. "I wonder where he is now?"

"He is—" Beverly began and was interrupted by the telephone.

"I'll get it!" Lenora swooped down upon the telephone and answered in her sweetest tones.

"Mike!" she exclaimed. "If that's not the strangest thing! We were just talking about you! Beverly? No, she hasn't. What's up? When did you get into town? Why haven't you— Mike? Mike!"

Slowly Lenora replaced the telephone and turned to the girls. "That's funny. He hung up on me."

"What did he say?" Beverly asked.

"Nothing," Lenora replied.

"You didn't give him a chance," Shirley laughed.

"He *did* ask me if Beverly said anything about him," Lenora remembered. "What did he mean, Bev?"

"He was at Lois's wedding this afternoon," Beverly explained, and went on to tell her friends about her conversation with Mike and the subsequent search she and Larry had made.

"We—we've got to do something," Lenora said, pacing up and down the room. "Mike is in a jam and we've got to help him out of it."

"We want to," Beverly agreed quickly. "If only he would tell us more about it. Perhaps he'll call again, Lenora. If he does, insist upon meeting him somewhere and then he can tell you the full story."

"I'll do my best," Lenora promised.

"Oh, I forgot. Larry and Terry are taking us out tonight," Beverly exclaimed. "Well, we'll come straight home after the show. If Mike calls in those few hours, surely he will call again."

"Well," Shirley sighed and got to her feet, "if Miss Dale Arden doesn't get moving, her show won't open tonight. My understudy is sick, so I *must* be there," she added. "I'll see you here after the show, and I hope you hear something more from Mike."

After Shirley had departed, Beverly and Lenora went to shower and dress for the evening. They listened anxiously, but the telephone remained silent. Mike did not call.

Throughout dinner with Larry and Terry, most of the conversation centered upon the gay, irrepressible Irishman. The new musical comedy they attended was sparkling and engrossing, and for a short time they almost forgot their anxiety about Mike. But immediately after the final curtain the girls insisted upon going home. From the street they could see that the apartment was dark.

"Shirley hasn't come home yet," Lenora commented.

"You didn't expect Mike to enter your apartment and put a light in the window, did you?" Terry demanded. Although he liked Mike and would do anything to help him, he considered him strong competition for Lenora's affections.

"I wonder if the telephone has been ringing," Lenora murmured, more to herself than to her companions.

"I'll call you tomorrow morning," Beverly told Larry, as they said good night. "Let me know if you hear anything."

Beverly and Lenora climbed the stairs to their apartment and then stopped short in surprise. Seated on a suitcase, and leaning against the door to their apartment, was a slender, well-dressed girl. At first they thought she had fallen asleep, but as they approached she sprang to her feet and flashed them a wide, charming smile.

"Hello," she said pleasantly. "I don't wonder you are surprised. I don't usually block traffic this way, but I thought it best to wait for you right here."

"You were waiting for us?" Lenora asked slowly.

"Yes," the girl said warmly. "You must be Lenora, and you—" she turned to the young reporter—"must be Beverly. I'd know you anywhere. I've come to stay with you."

CHAPTER III

The Search Is Begun

BEVERLY and Lenora stood and stared at the black-haired girl. Her dark eyes returned their stare with dismay.

"Didn't Lois tell you I was coming? Where is Lois, by the way?"

"She was married this afternoon and is at present on an airliner en route to Africa," Lenora answered. "And she didn't tell us about you, Miss—"

"My name is Betsy Fuller—" the girl began.

"Wait!" Beverly interrupted. "Let's go in where we can be more comfortable."

Beverly unlocked the door to the girls' apartment and went ahead, lighting lamps and drawing shades, while Lenora helped Betsy with her suitcase.

Shirley arrived just as the girls were seating themselves, and she, too, listened in surprise as Betsy told her brief story.

"I'm from a small town near Chicago. I've known Lois for years. She told my sister and me that we could stay here whenever we came to New York. I arrived tonight and came directly here. I don't know anyone else in New York. Didn't Lois tell you *anything* about me or my sister?"

"No, she didn't!" Lenora said bluntly.

"This is most embarrassing," Betsy declared. "I was sure Lois would be here, otherwise—" She broke off unhappily. "If you can recommend a small hotel—"

"What did you come to New York for?" Shirley asked. "Is it a vacation trip?"

"Oh no! I plan to find a job," Betsy said at once. "I had hoped Lois could advise me about things, but now—" She looked ready to cry.

The three Alpha Delta girls looked at each other and then back at their guest.

"Don't you know anyone else at all in New York?" Beverly asked gently.

"Not a soul," Betsy assured them tragically. "I had counted on Lois—" With a sigh, she stood up. "I'll go now. I'm sorry I bothered you."

"Where are you going?" Lenora wanted to know.

"Oh—a hotel, I guess," the girl replied.

"Nonsense!" Lenora said crisply. "You can't go any-where alone at this hour. You can have Lois's bed for the night, can't she, girls?"

Beverly and Shirley nodded.

"You mean I can stay here?" Betsy looked delighted. "I promise I won't bother you. If you'll just let me stay with you for a day or two until I get acquainted with New York and have a job in view—"

"I meant for tonight," Lenora exclaimed. "But—well —I guess a few days will be all right. It's strange Lois didn't tell us about you."

"I suppose she was so busy with her wedding plans that she had no time to think about poor little me," Betsy said, smiling.

"I suppose so," Lenora agreed. "Well, bring your things into the bedroom. I'll help you get settled."

"What do you think, Bev?" Shirley whispered, following her friend into the kitchen.

"About Betsy? She seems nice enough," Beverly answered.

"I agree with Lenora that it is strange Lois didn't tell us about her," Shirley said.

"You're always telling me my newspaper work makes me overly suspicious of people sometimes," Beverly teased. "Who's suspicious now?"

"I am," Shirley admitted, "but don't you agree that Lois should have told us about her?"

"Yes, I do," Beverly said, "but let's give Betsy a chance. One can't always rely on first impressions."

"Oh, my first impression was all right," Shirley replied, "but after she started talking—" She broke off, shaking her head.

Betsy chatted gaily as the girls prepared to go to bed. At last the three friends dropped off to sleep, but Betsy lay awake, smiling into the darkness.

The next morning found Betsy making herself right at home. She was up before the other girls and had breakfast almost ready by the time they finished dressing.

"We didn't expect such service," Lenora said, beaming at the plate of hot muffins Betsy placed on the table. "Where did you learn to cook like this?"

"My mother taught me," Betsy told her, smiling. "I hope you don't mind my making myself at home this way."

"Of course not!" Lenora mumbled, her mouth full. "These muffins are out of this world! You should make a career of cooking!"

Betsy laughed and changed the subject.

"Tell me about the careers you girls have. What do you do, Lenora?"

Breakfast time turned into a question-and-answer game, with Betsy doing the questioning and learning a great deal about the girls and their friends.

Afterwards, Shirley commented on it when the three Alpha Delta girls were alone in the kitchen.

"She means well," Lenora defended. "And wasn't that a good breakfast?"

"So she can scramble an egg." Shirley shrugged. "Who can't?"

"An egg, yes," Lenora grinned, "but none of us makes

muffins like the ones she made. You're being unfair, Shirley. It's natural that she is interested in us as Lois's friends."

"I think she asks too many questions," Shirley insisted. "Did you notice that she told us very little about herself?"

"What is she doing now?" Beverly asked.

Lenora peeped into the living room.

"She's looking at the photograph album you keep on your desk," the blonde girl reported.

"See what I mean?" Shirley demanded. "She had no right to help herself to Beverly's book."

"She is only looking at the pictures," Lenora sighed. "Do you mind, Bev?"

"No," Beverly said. "She may look at it all she likes. I think I'll telephone Larry and see if he has any news of Mike."

"Perhaps this is a case where no news is good news," Lenora added hopefully. "I wonder why he didn't call me back."

Beverly entered the living room and crossed to her desk. Betsy did not hear her coming, and when Beverly stopped beside her Betsy jumped back with a muffled exclamation.

"You startled me! I thought you were busy in the kitchen. I hope you don't mind my looking at your album. I love pictures."

Beverly had seen her staring at a group picture taken when the girls and their friends had been cruising on the yacht *Susabella*. Now she commented upon it.

"I know." Betsy smiled. "I've seen this picture before. It is very good—of all of you."

Later Beverly was to recall that innocent remark and wonder why her suspicions had not been aroused then.

Larry had heard nothing from Mike during the night, but he had not given up hope. He was still determined to learn how he could help his friend, and he declared his intention of visiting the man whom Mike was accused of robbing.

"I'll get in to see him somehow!" Larry vowed.

"I'm going with you," Beverly said. "Meet me in front of the *Tribune* office."

"It must be exciting to be a reporter," Betsy sighed when Beverly turned away from the telephone. "Are you off on a good story?"

"I hope it is a good one," Beverly said.

"I couldn't help overhearing what you said," Betsy apologized. "You asked someone about news of Mike. Is it the same Mike who is in this picture?"

"Yes," Lenora said, joining them at that moment. "He has gotten himself in trouble again."

"Oh?" Betsy was interested immediately. "What sort of trouble?"

"We aren't sure of the details yet," Beverly put in. "Ready, Lenora?"

"As ready for work as I ever am," Lenora said. "Will you be all right, Betsy?"

"Oh, yes!" Betsy assured her brightly. "Shirley can

tell me all about the play she's in, and then perhaps I'll go out for a walk. See you tonight!"

Beverly reported to her editor, along with Lenora, who was building up a good reputation as a press photographer. Charlie Blaine had given Beverly her first job when she graduated from college and he had never had cause to regret it. He was proud of the way she had developed into a first-class reporter, and now he trusted her with more important assignments.

When Beverly told him about Mike, Blaine showed definite interest. He had met Mike through Beverly and Lenora, and had liked the young man. Also, he thought that behind Mike's predicament might be a good story. He consented to Beverly following through on it, but Lenora he assigned to take pictures of a political rally for another reporter.

"I'll tell you what we find out," Beverly soothed her friend, as Lenora, disappointed, followed her out of Charlie Blaine's office. "We won't find Mike in Mr. Brewster's office, you know."

Lenora refused to be comforted.

"I want to help Mike. How can I do it taking pictures of some pompous—"

"Temper, temper!" Beverly laughed. "I'll meet you here for lunch and reveal all."

Beverly hurried off to meet Larry, and together they drove to the address they had copied from the telephone directory the day before. It proved to be a secluded brownstone house in the East Sixties.

"I hope Mr. Brewster is home today," Beverly commented as Larry parked the car in front of the house.

"I hope he feels like talking about the robbery," Larry added. "We can't actually do anything until we learn the details and find out what really happened."

They left the car and approached the door. The windows were all closed, and there was no sign of anyone. Beverly rang the doorbell.

The butler who opened the door to them said Mr. Brewster was not at home to anyone. However, Larry persuaded him to take the message that they were friends of Michael McKay, and it brought an instant response.

"If you will follow me, please—"

The butler led the way to a pine-paneled library where a stocky, sandy-haired man sat behind a huge desk, busily poring over a miscellany of papers. He looked up when they entered and greeted them with a frown.

"What do you know about Michael McKay?" he demanded abruptly.

"Is it true that he is suspected of having robbed you?" Larry demanded with equal briskness.

"Not suspected," was the retort. "I *know* he did it. Who are you?"

"I'm Larry Owens. I went to college with Mike," Larry answered. "This is Miss Beverly Gray—"

"From the *Tribune*?" Mr. Brewster demanded suspiciously.

"Yes," Beverly admitted.

"I've seen your by-line," Mr. Brewster stated and turned back to the work on his desk. "I have nothing to say to any reporters. Good day. Tyson will show you out."

CHAPTER IV

The Victim

THE butler coughed discreetly behind them, but they ignored him. Neither of them gave up so easily.

"I came here because I, too, am a friend of Mike's," Beverly said firmly. "We do not believe he is a thief."

"And we ask that you prove it," Larry added challengingly.

"The police are at this moment searching for Michael McKay, and when he is found he will be prosecuted to the full extent of the law," Mr. Brewster informed them coldly. "And now—good day!"

"Mike is not a thief!" Beverly exclaimed. "Mr. Brewster—please! Tell us what he did and give us a chance to defend him."

"How can you defend a man who has betrayed his employer's confidence and trust?" Mr. Brewster wanted to know. "I have nothing to say for publication."

"Nothing will be published until you give me your consent," Beverly assured him. "As Mike's friend, I want to hear what he is accused of."

"Very well." Mr. Brewster threw down his pen and leaned back in his chair. "I shall tell you the whole story—from the very beginning. Then you can judge for yourselves. Tyson, bring us some coffee."

The butler withdrew and Mr. Brewster waved Beverly and Larry toward chairs.

"Mike and I were out in Montana—in the northern part among the mountains. We were looking for gold deposits. During the long weeks of our search we became firm friends—or so I thought. I won't describe all the disappointments we had, but it was a rugged trip in more ways than one. Then, just when we were about to give up, we found it—the richest deposit uncovered in many years. It will take a lot of work to reach it, but our company has a great many resources. However, that is not part of the story.

"For several days I had been running a temperature. All the climbing among the rocky foothills, as well as the hot sun, was too much for me. On our way back to the camp we had established, as I was scrambling down the rocky cliff, I slipped and fell. I would have gone over the edge, probably to my death, but for Mike. How he did it I will never know, but he caught hold of me and held on. Slowly he pulled me back to where I could get my footing. He saved my life."

"Yet you accuse him of being a thief?" Larry asked softly.

Mr. Brewster made no reply to that, but went on with his story.

"In my fall I had badly twisted the muscles of my leg and within the hour it began to swell. I could not put my weight on it, and it was agony to move it. That, together with my fever, really laid me low.

"Mike took me back to the little town of Red Camp where we had our headquarters. The doctor there did what he could for me, and then Mike arranged to have me flown home while he went back and continued his work at our discovery point. He had to make a map of the terrain, stake out our claim points, negotiate for rights of way for our heavy equipment—there were a hundred details to take care of."

"Mike had your okay to do all this, didn't he?" Larry put in.

John Brewster nodded. "I trusted him implicitly. I left everything in his hands. I suppose it was then that the idea occurred to him."

"What idea?" Beverly asked.

"The idea to keep the gold for himself," Mr. Brewster answered heavily. For the first time, Beverly realized that Mr. Brewster's anger at Mike was mixed with hurt.

"He would hardly change so quickly," Beverly commented, "when you found him perfectly honest before."

"Gold can be a terrible temptation," Mr. Brewster

said, "and we had been through weeks of disappointment and discouragement."

"Tell us what Mike did next," Larry probed.

"He drew detailed maps of the region, bought the necessary land with company funds I had put at his disposal, and then brought all the papers here to me."

"Why would he do that if he planned to steal the gold discovery for himself?" Beverly asked.

Mr. Brewster shrugged. "I don't know what his idea was."

"Tell us what happened then," Larry urged. "When was the robbery?"

"The day Mike arrived, I had invited my secretary and her brother to dinner and I asked Mike to join us. It was a pleasant evening. We played bridge for a while after dinner and then Mike excused himself and left early. When my guests had gone, I came into the library intending to study the papers Mike had brought that afternoon. The desk had been thoroughly searched, one drawer broken open, and all the papers stolen."

"That doesn't prove it was Mike who took them," Beverly said.

"I called Inspector Travers, who is a personal friend of mine. He and his fingerprint experts came, and went over the desk carefully. The only fingerprints, other than mine, which were on the drawer that had been broken into were Mike's. He must have come in here and taken the papers while the rest of us were at the bridge table. No wonder he had to leave early!"

"Who else was here that evening?" Larry asked.

"I've told you—my secretary, who was leaving on a month's vacation, and her brother, whom I had interviewed for a position with our company."

"During the bridge game, when your secretary or her brother was dummy, did either of them leave the room?" Larry continued.

"Yes," Mr. Brewster said thoughtfully. "My secretary went to get a handkerchief from her coat pocket, and her brother went out once to make a telephone call."

"In other words," Beverly said, "either of them could have come in here, taken the papers, and rejoined the game."

"But Mike's fingerprints were the ones found on the drawer," John Brewster pointed out. "Furthermore, if he didn't steal the papers, why has he gone into hiding?"

"You might find him through publicity," Beverly said. "Why have you kept the robbery such a secret?"

"I asked Inspector Travers to avoid publicity for fear it might start a rush to the gold territory," John Brewster replied, "though the gold is inaccessible to most people. It is going to take all the resources of our mining company to bring it out."

"In that case, how would Mike profit by the plans? He doesn't have a large mining company, other than yours, interested in his work."

"How do you know?" Mr. Brewster demanded. "He may have been working secretly for another company all this time. Such things have happened before. He must have accomplices. He might have used me and my knowledge to find the gold, and planned to betray me when he had all the information."

"Why should he bring the papers to you if that were his plan?" Beverly wanted to know. "Why didn't he just disappear in Montana?"

"I believe he planned to make the robbery look like someone else's work but was interrupted before he could erase his fingerprints," Mr. Brewster replied.

"Mike wouldn't do such a thing," Larry protested. "I've had several letters in which he spoke of you with the greatest respect and admiration."

"Even if he did take the papers," Beverly said slowly, "you own the property and rights of way. No one else can work the mine."

Mr. Brewster shook his head.

"When Mike negotiated for the land he bought it in his own name. He said it was easier to transact the business that way. He intended to transfer all the titles to the company as soon as he returned east. We didn't have time to take care of it. Mike still has title to the land. Of course I will fight him in court, but it may take months—" Mr. Brewster looked grim. "I've been the victim of a very clever thief."

"I still don't believe Mike would betray your trust that way," Larry insisted. "I don't think things are as bad as you think."

"Nor do I," Beverly agreed firmly.

"I shall find out," Mr. Brewster said harshly. "To use the maps and get the gold he must return to Red Camp. I intend to go to the gold site and wait for him!"

CHAPTER V

Questions Without Answers

LENORA had not returned from her assignment when Beverly got back to the *Tribune* office, but she came in while her friend was talking to Charlie Blaine about Mike, and immediately joined them.

"There's a story there all right," Blaine was saying. "There is more than personal greed behind Mike's actions."

"No one would be so careless as to leave his fingerprints like that," Beverly said, frowning. "There must be an explanation. If he were guilty, wouldn't he have tried to throw suspicion upon someone else—not directly upon himself?"

"That's your job—find out," Blaine said.

"Mr. Brewster is going to Montana to wait until Mike

comes to the gold site," Beverly told him. "He is pretty sure Mike will come."

"Then go there too," Blaine directed. "Stick with him until you find Mike and get the story."

"If Beverly goes looking for Mike, I'm going too," Lenora put in firmly.

"I've other assignments for you," Blaine replied.

"Please, Mr. Blaine," Lenora begged. "This is important to me. I want to find Mike. Besides, Bev ought not to go alone."

"You are really fond of Mike, aren't you?" Blaine inquired with a smile. "Very well, Lenora, go with Beverly, but you better take some good pictures!"

"Now," Lenora urged, when the two girls left the editor's office, "tell me all that Mr. Brewster said."

"Wait—" Beverly answered, "my telephone is ringing."

It was Larry.

"I've just talked to Mr. Brewster again, on the phone." Larry told her. "I persuaded him to let me accompany him to Red Camp."

"I want to go too," Beverly said. "So does Lenora."

"I don't think he will agree to that," Larry returned. "He assured me it is no pleasure trip and he is not going to make a party of it. He is letting me go along only because of my friendship for Mike. Secretly, I think, he wants to believe Mike is innocent."

"We're Mike's friends, too," Beverly said. "I'm going to ask him."

Beverly succeeded in getting John Brewster on the telephone, and she explained her desire. He was adamant. No amount of persuasive talk on her part changed his mind.

"Positively not, Miss Gray! The country out there is rugged, and we may be there for weeks. This is not going to be a pleasure jaunt. We are after a thief. Mr. Owens and I shall go alone."

He hung up and Beverly turned to face Lenora.

" 'Positively not, Miss Gray!' " she mimicked. "As far as he is concerned, the matter is closed."

"But not as far as we are concerned," Lenora declared. "Am I right?"

Beverly laughed.

"Right, as usual. But first I'm going to talk to Inspector Travers. He knows John Brewster and he covered the robbery."

"Fortunately, he's our friend, too," Lenora said happily.

The two girls went to see the police officer whom they knew well from previous meetings in their newspaper work. They found him reluctant to listen to their questions or to discuss John Brewster and the robbery. It was not until Beverly told him of seeing Mike the day before that the inspector became interested.

"If you know his present whereabouts you should tell me, Miss Gray. After all, he is wanted for questioning—"

"Only for questioning?" Beverly interrupted.

"Well, we feel he *is* the thief," Inspector Travers admitted. "What evidence there is points to his guilt."

"Mike is not a thief," Lenora put in stanchly. "I'm sure he can explain everything."

"It will take a lot of explaining to brush aside those fingerprints of his," the inspector said bluntly. "If he is innocent, why doesn't he come forward and tell us what happened? I repeat, Miss Gray, if you know his whereabouts it is your duty to tell me. Withholding information about a wanted criminal—"

"Don't talk about Mike like that!" Lenora protested.

"I don't know where he is now," Beverly said. "He disappeared after telling me not to believe he is guilty. Larry and I tried to find him but had no success."

The inspector sighed. "You two are emotionally involved because Mike is your friend," he stated flatly. "To us—Mike is a man who has committed a crime, and we want to find him."

"That was a waste of time," Lenora said distastefully when the girls emerged again into the afternoon sunshine. "If only Mike hadn't run away! What do we do now, Bev?"

"There were two other people at John Brewster's that night," Beverly said. "I'm going to his office and ask about his secretary."

"She is away on vacation—or so he said," Lenora reminded her friend.

"Maybe someone there can tell me where to reach her brother," Beverly said.

They found the ultramodern offices of the Brewster Mining Company without difficulty. The receptionist was pleasant when they approached her with their questions.

"Miss Jones is away on vacation," she said. "She sailed for Bermuda yesterday."

"Is her brother employed here?" Beverly asked.

"Not yet. Are you friends of hers?" the girl asked as she considered them smilingly.

"Oh, yes," Lenora assured her innocently. "Though we haven't seen her for some time."

"She has been trying to get Stephen a job with our company," the receptionist confided. "She and Steve had dinner with Mr. Brewster to discuss it the night before she sailed, but I haven't heard what Mr. Brewster's decision was."

"Can you tell us where we could locate Stephen?" Beverly asked.

"Oh, he sailed with her," was the reply. "I suppose when they return he will have a job with us."

"How long will they be gone?" Lenora wanted to know.

"A month."

"Do you know Michael McKay?" Beverly asked next.

"Mike? Oh, yes! It's too bad about him. I never thought he would turn out to be a thief."

"Oh, then you know about the robbery," Beverly said. "I thought Mr. Brewster was keeping it a secret."

The receptionist shrugged. "You know how gossip is. Bad news travels fast. I always liked Mike. He was very popular with everyone in the office."

"Do you really think he did it?" Lenora probed.

"I heard they have proof that he did. How did you two hear about it?" the girl asked suspiciously.

"We are friends of Mike's," Beverly said.

"Oh!" The receptionist looked them over thoughtfully and her friendly manner cooled perceptibly. "Do you wish to speak with anyone else in the office?"

"No, thank you," Beverly said.

The two friends left the mining company office with the receptionist staring after them.

"Did you notice how she changed when we said we were friends of Mike?" Lenora said angrily. "Poor Mike! He isn't getting a fair chance to defend himself. We simply must find him!"

"Then we will have to go west with Mr. Brewster," Beverly said simply. "It's the only chance we have."

From Larry, Beverly learned Mr. Brewster's plans of departure and the girls planned theirs to coincide with his.

At the apartment they found Betsy Fuller very much interested in the trip they were undertaking. They told her some of their plans, but not all the details, and said very little about Mike. Her manner of asking questions sometimes annoyed them, and they began to wish they had not been so free with their hospitality.

"Live and learn," Lenora muttered, bending over her

suitcase. "I certainly hope she will find a job soon and another place to live."

"So do I," Shirley whispered. "I'll be alone with her after you gals are gone."

"Poor Shirley," Beverly sympathized, smiling.

"Send us a blow-by-blow description of how you get along," added Lenora.

"Lenora's wanted on the telephone," Betsy announced from the bedroom doorway. "It's a man and he has the nicest voice—"

Beverly and Shirley exchanged amused glances. Betsy could become rapturous over the slightest hint of romance.

"It was Terry," Lenora reported when she returned. "He wanted to know about our plans for the week end. I told him I was going out of town on an assignment."

"Did you tell him where you're going?" Shirley asked.

"Not exactly," Lenora answered. "I was afraid he might want to go along."

"Does he know Mike, too?" Betsy wanted to know.

"Yes, he does," Lenora answered shortly.

"Where shall we forward your mail while you're gone?" Betsy continued helpfully.

"Send it in care of General Delivery, Red Camp, Montana," Beverly replied.

"Where is *that?*" Betsy demanded in bewilderment.

"The mailman will find it—probably faster than we will," Lenora said dryly.

"If you don't know where it is, why go there?" Betsy asked wonderingly.

Lenora, ignoring the question, said abruptly, "Bev, have you seen my jodhpurs?"

"They are at the back of your closet," Shirley told her.

"May I borrow your binoculars for the trip?" Lenora asked Shirley. "Something about mountains always makes me want binoculars."

"Help yourself," Shirley said generously.

"What time tomorrow does your train leave?" Betsy asked. "Shirley and I will go to the station with you."

"That isn't necessary," Beverly said. "It will be just the time when Shirley must be on her way to the theater. We'll take a taxi."

"Oh, but I love to see people off on trips," Betsy said enthusiastically. "Please let me come! Poor little me, I never get to go anywhere."

There was no way of knowing how long they would be gone. It could be two weeks or several. As the time of departure drew nearer, a note of excitement began to make itself felt.

"I hope Mike isn't too anxious to return to New York when we find him," Lenora confided to Beverly. "We could all have a wonderful vacation."

"I've always loved the West," Beverly agreed.

"Wide open spaces, tall trees and mountains, cowboys—" Lenora grinned. "I hope it hasn't changed since the last time we were there."

"We've never been in that section of the country," Beverly returned. "From what Mr. Brewster told us, it sounds like wild and unsettled country."

"I can hardly wait." Lenora shivered ecstatically.

When it came time to leave the apartment, they said good-bye there to Shirley, who had to hurry to the theater. But Betsy insisted upon accompanying them in the taxi.

They bought magazines and candy at the newsstand in the station and hurried toward the track on which their train waited.

"I hope you find your friend soon," Betsy said in farewell.

"We hope so, too," Lenora replied. "We'll send you a postcard."

As they hurried through the gate after the porter who was carrying their luggage, Beverly happened to look back. She saw Betsy approach a man, tuck her arm within his, and hurry away with him. The girls were too far away to be able to distinguish his features.

"I thought she didn't know anyone in New York," Lenora, who had turned to see if Beverly was coming, commented in surprise.

"That was her story," Beverly agreed.

"I thought that 'poor little me' routine was a bit thick," Lenora said. "When we get back I'm going to have a little chat with that young lady."

"Perhaps we should have cabled Lois," Beverly commented. "Perhaps we were too trusting."

"You mean you suspect that Lois never knew her?" Lenora demanded, hurrying along beside her companion. "But then who is she? How did she know about us? Oh dear! We're going all the way to Montana to solve a mystery when all the time we have one in our own apartment."

"Look!" Beverly drew Lenora aside. "Here come Mr. Brewster and Larry."

Larry had agreed to keep the girls' plans secret from Mr. Brewster until they were all on the train en route to the West. Once or twice Larry had mentioned Beverly and her desire to join them, and each time Mr. Brewster had been as stubbornly against it as when he had talked with Beverly. The young people finally decided not to say any more until the girls were well on their way and he could not stop them.

"When do you plan to meet him?" Lenora whispered.

"Tonight at dinner," Beverly said. "Larry is going to arrange with the dining car steward to seat them at a table for four. Then we will stroll in and join them."

"And be tossed right out again," Lenora said, following Beverly on board the train. "Mr. Brewster looks mighty formidable to me."

"His bark is worse than his bite," Beverly assured her. "How do you like our compartment?"

Lenora sank down on a seat and closed her eyes with a sigh.

"I am going to love every minute of this trip—in

spite of worry about Mike. We haven't been away for so long—"

Beverly laughed and sat down beside her friend.

"Is your wanderlust troubling you again?"

"It certainly is!" Lenora exclaimed. "What time is it? When do we eat? Why couldn't you have arranged to meet Mr. Brewster after dinner? I'm afraid he'll spoil my appetite."

"It won't be long," Beverly consoled. "Read your magazine while we're waiting."

The train began to move and they settled themselves comfortably. Soon it was time to freshen up and make their way to the dining car.

Larry and Mr. Brewster were already seated, and when Beverly spoke to the steward he showed the girls to the men's table.

"Miss Gray! What are you doing on this train?" Mr. Brewster demanded, rising to his feet. "I thought I made it quite clear that your presence was not needed on this trip."

"Mr. Brewster, please—" Beverly began.

"Either you leave the train at the next station or I shall," he continued coldly.

"Beverly dear, what is this gentleman getting so excited about?" Lenora drawled, ignoring the man across the table. "Tell him that anyone who pays the fare may ride on the train. It's a free country. Besides, Mr. Blaine would not be at all pleased if we returned without pictures and stories from our western vacation.

This gentleman—did you say his name was Mr. Brewster?—might receive some very unfavorable publicity if we were forced off the train."

"You are quite right, Lenora," Beverly agreed, trying hard not to smile. Out of the corner of her eye she saw Larry's grin about to burst forth at Lenora's hauteur.

"This is blackmail!" Mr. Brewster sputtered angrily.

"It would be better to have us on your side," Lenora agreed cheerfully.

Mr. Brewster shook his head helplessly and threw up his hands.

"I know when I am defeated," he said in sudden capitulation. "What is your name, young lady?"

"This is Lenora Whitehill," Larry introduced.

"Oh, that explains it," Mr. Brewster exclaimed. "Mike told me about you."

"What did he tell you?" Lenora asked suspiciously.

"That must remain a secret between Mike and me," Mr. Brewster answered with a chuckle.

From that moment on, the four were on polite, if not exactly friendly, terms. They discussed the aspects of their trip, and tried to anticipate what Mike would do. With every mile traveled they became more anxious to reach their destination.

"We should have flown west," Lenora commented as she and Beverly retired to their compartment the second night. "We would have been there in a matter of hours."

"Mr. Brewster doesn't like to fly," Beverly answered.

"That's funny," Lenora said. "What he said when he heard my name is funny, too. I wonder what Mike told him about me?"

"Maybe Mike will tell us when we find him," Beverly said as she snapped out the light.

CHAPTER VI·

Red Camp

THE bus ride from Colber, where they left the train, to the little town of Red Camp served to remind them of the natural scenic wonders and vast unsettled regions of their busy country. The sky overhead was a cloudless blue, and the air was cool and pine-scented. Mountains lined the horizon like jealous guardians of the valleys at their feet. Green fields and forests lay on both sides of the road, and occasionally small animals scurried out of sight.

"I love it," Lenora declared, stretching to get a clearer view of the mountains. "I only wish there was better transportation," she added as the bus hit a bump in the road and they were jolted violently.

"The bus service has just started," Mr. Brewster told them.

"This is a bus?" Lenora demanded caustically. "I feel as though I'm riding in a cement mixer."

"This particular vehicle has seen better days," Mr. Brewster admitted. "It was converted from school service, and serves to carry mail and passengers from the railroad station at Colber to Red Camp and four or five other communities farther north. It makes two round trips each day."

"If Mike is in Red Camp, he must have come this way," Lenora exclaimed. "Ask the driver!"

"I already have," Larry assured her. "He hasn't had any strangers as passengers for two weeks."

"Mike would be too cautious to use a public means of transportation," added Mr. Brewster. "He might hire a car or a horse. He is quite fond of riding. We used horses when we were here before. He had a little cow pony named Lady that he loved. I'm surprised he didn't buy her and take her east with him."

"She wouldn't have fitted into his apartment," Lenora replied.

"How much farther is it to Red Camp?" Beverly asked.

"We should be there in about ten minutes," Mr. Brewster answered. "If you have noticed, the road has been climbing steadily. When we reach the next crest you will be able to see Red Camp in the valley below."

The narrow, winding road reached the summit, and spread out below them they could see a green valley broken by a thread of silver where a mountain stream rushed from the foothills. A group of small, wooden buildings stood in the center of the valley.

"That is Red Camp," Mr. Brewster indicated. "It isn't much, is it?"

"Much?" Lenora echoed. "It isn't anything! I thought such places existed only in cowboy movies!"

"Red Camp was originally settled by a group of gold seekers. The foothills are dotted with abandoned mines. The gold proved too scarce and difficult to obtain. But now that we know it *is* there, today's mining equipment can obtain it."

"That's where your company comes in," Larry said.

"Yes, providing we can find Mike and clear up the mess he has made," Mr. Brewster said unhappily.

The bus rattled to an abrupt halt before a two-story wooden building. In faded white letters a sign above the door read: "Hotel."

"There is a restaurant across the street, next to the local jail and sheriff's office; a general store, a church, schoolhouse, and a garage," Mr. Brewster said.

"Where are the homes and people?" Lenora wanted to know.

"There's a row of homes on the next street," Mr. Brewster explained, "but most people come in from farms and ranches. About a mile out of town is a large dude ranch that is quite popular in the summer."

"I suppose Red Camp has been left in this undeveloped condition to give local color for the summer visitors," Larry smiled.

"That has a lot to do with it," Mr. Brewster agreed. "Let's go in and see about our rooms."

The interior of the hotel was clean and cool, after the dusty ride on the bus, and the girls were shown to a small but neat room overlooking the street. Mr. Brewster and Larry shared a room across the hall.

After they had unpacked some of their things and freshened up, they met in the lobby and Mr. Brewster led the way across the street to the restaurant for dinner.

"The Gold Nugget Café," Lenora read from the menu. "I love this place. It is so—so—atmospherish."

"That's a good word," Larry laughed. "I suppose we may see Billy the Kid come in at any minute."

"To play the juke box," Beverly added with a laugh.

"Mr. Brewster!" a booming voice exclaimed behind them, and they turned to see a huge, red-faced, jovial man bearing down on them.

"This is Pete—the owner of the place," Mr. Brewster explained.

The two men greeted each other like old friends. Introductions were made and dinner ordered. Pete lingered to talk with them while they tasted the thick steak the waitress placed before them.

"Have you seen Mike lately?" Mr. Brewster asked his friend.

"The young fellow who was with you on your last trip?" Pete asked. "No. He left here over a week ago. He said his work was finished."

"I expect him to return," Mr. Brewster said. "If you see him, let me know at once—but don't tell him I'm here. I want to surprise him."

Pete agreed and wandered away to the kitchen.

"We must have gotten here before Mike," Lenora commented.

"I hope we haven't made a wrong guess." Larry frowned. "Suppose he doesn't come?"

"The gold is here. He will come," Mr. Brewster said firmly. "There is one more man I want to talk to about him—Greg Holden. He owns the dude ranch where we can hire horses."

"Let's go to see him now," Larry proposed. "How do you get there? Is it far?"

"We'll rent a car at the garage and drive out to the ranch," Mr. Brewster answered. "It will only take a few minutes."

The Double-O Ranch was a beautiful spot, made so with a desire to impress the tourist trade as being authentically western. A huge wagon wheel, painted sparkling white, stood on each side of the entrance to the gravel drive leading to the low, rambling ranch house. This was also white against a background of green trees. The huge barn and stables, too, were white, as were the corral fence and hitching post.

While Mr. Brewster and Larry went to the house to talk to Mr. Holden, Beverly and Lenora wandered down to the corral where a group of horses was assembled.

"Mr. Brewster said we would rent horses to explore the countryside looking for Mike," Lenora commented. "Let's pick the ones you and I want now."

Beverly leaned on the top rail of the corral fence and pointed to a brown-and-white pony standing to one side staring at them.

"I want that one," Beverly said at once. "She is a beauty."

"It didn't take you long to decide," Lenora commented. "Let's see—I wonder if that black one is gentle?"

"He would toss you off in two seconds," drawled a voice behind them.

A young man in dungarees and plaid shirt and wearing the customary ten-gallon hat halted beside them.

"Are you aiming to hire a couple of horses?" he inquired.

"I reckon we are," Lenora drawled, eyes twinkling. "What ones would you suggest?"

"Have you ever been on a horse before?" he asked, looking them over shrewdly.

"We have," Lenora nodded, "but not for some time," she added truthfully.

"Then I'd say you would about suit Red over there," the man replied. "He is the laziest critter—he wouldn't work up enough steam to throw anyone off."

"I might suit him, but will he suit me?" Lenora retorted. "After all, I don't want one that will go to sleep when I'm riding him."

The man lifted the rope from the gatepost and motioned her to enter the corral.

"Come and see if you get along together," he invited.

The reddish-brown horse called Red cocked his ears as Lenora approached. With one foot he pawed the ground and nodded his head vigorously.

Lenora reached out and he let her stroke his nose. As she turned aside he nuzzled her gently and she resumed her petting.

"He likes you," the man commented. "He is a ladies' man." He turned to Beverly. "I think you would like Tony here, miss."

"I would rather have that brown-and-white pony," Beverly replied, her mind made up.

"Tony is gentle," the cowboy assured her, "and he knows the hills around here better than a lot of people. You couldn't get lost on him."

"Isn't she gentle?" Beverly asked, indicating her choice.

"Yes," the man said slowly. "She is the smartest one of the lot, but she hasn't been feeling so chipper lately. She is lonely, I guess."

"Lonely!" Lenora echoed. "With all these horses?"

"A young fellow from the East had her for several weeks," the man explained. "He made a regular pet out of her, and ever since he went away she has sort of been—well—pining for him."

"What is her name?" Beverly asked, feeling that she already knew.

"That is Lady," the man answered. "Mr. McKay said that when he came out here again he would want to ride her and no other. It is as if she understood and is waiting for him."

"I want her," Beverly insisted. "If Mr. McKay comes for her, I will, of course, be glad to turn her over to him. We are staying at the hotel in town. He can see me there."

Beverly hoped that Mike's horse might serve as another bit of bait to lure him out into the open where they could see and talk with him.

CHAPTER VII

Trapped

THE next morning they had an early breakfast and rode out to the Double-O Ranch where their horses were saddled and waiting. The ranch cook also provided an excellent picnic lunch, and they started out eagerly to find another man whom Mr. Brewster wanted to see.

"Old Ben was very friendly with Mike when we were here," Mr. Brewster explained. "He helped us a lot with stories of old mines. Greg Holden said that after I left, Mike stayed with Ben for several days. If Mike does come here, I'm sure he will get in touch with Ben."

Mr. Brewster led the way into the foothills, on narrow trails away from the highway that joined one community to the next.

"This will help refresh my memory, too," he said as they rode. "To reach the actual gold site, we will have to make at least a two-day journey and camp out. I don't believe I will have much trouble taking you to our old camp site, but as to actually finding the gold again—I am not so sure. My illness made my memory vague on where we went that last day, and I did not have time to study the maps Mike brought back."

"Did you survey all this countryside?" Larry asked.

"We concentrated mostly on the spots where old gold strikes had been made. We went through a dozen abandoned mines. We found traces of gold in the creek we will soon see, but we believe now it must have come from the rocks over which the water travels as it comes through the foothills. Gold deposits, such as the one we found, are difficult to locate, because the gold is usually distributed through the rock formation in small particles. Where the gold has been deposited in river beds it is not so difficult to find. There we could use a magnetometer to find it.

"I remember one thing about our discovery—it was very rocky country, and dominating the spot where we found the gold were two columns of rock. I dreamed about them when I got back to New York. It was the one thing I could remember clearly out of the nightmare of that last day. In silhouette, the rocks looked just like pine trees, and Mike said he would draw his map around the 'twin pines,' as he called them."

They ate their lunch seated on a carpet of pine needles under the spreading branches of huge, ancient trees. A cool, shallow creek gurgled past on its way to the valley, and around them the breeze whispered through the trees.

"Think," Lenora sighed, "just a few days ago we stood on Fifth Avenue dodging traffic, never dreaming such a peaceful spot existed."

As they talked Beverly noticed a shadow pass between the trees behind Lenora. At first she thought she had imagined it, but a moment later the branches of a bush moved although the breeze had died down.

"Someone is watching us from the bushes," Beverly whispered to Larry. "He is right behind Lenora."

"You go to one side and I'll go to the other," Larry returned softly. "Try to surprise him."

Beverly and Larry sauntered past the blonde girl and suddenly dashed into the bushes in a vain attempt to encircle the spy. Beverly was unrewarded by even a glimpse of him, but Larry was bowled over by a running figure which appeared and disappeared with such suddenness he scarcely knew what hit him.

"What's going on?" Lenora demanded as she and Mr. Brewster ran up to where Larry was dusting himself off.

"Beverly saw someone lurking in the bushes. We tried to head him off, but he was too fast," Larry explained.

"Maybe it was a bear," Lenora said hopefully. "I

would love to have a bear rug. Let's go after him."

"I doubt if it was a bear," Mr. Brewster laughed. "It might have been a deer."

"What I saw didn't have antlers," Beverly said firmly. "It was a man."

"Why would anyone spy on us?" Lenora inquired. "We are perfectly harmless."

"Anyway, he is gone now," Beverly smiled. "Suppose we fill our canteens and be on our way?"

Larry and Mr. Brewster filled the canteens and they prepared to mount. Before they left, Lenora decided to wash the remnants of a chocolate bar from her fingers, and ran down to the edge of the creek. A moment later, her friends heard her scream.

"What happened? Was it a snake?" Beverly cried.

Lenora shook her head, and pointed a shaking finger at the creek water.

"It was there! I leaned over to wash my hands, and the most awful face was right there in the water—staring at me!"

"The creek isn't deep enough for anyone to be in swimming," Larry observed. "Maybe you saw a fish."

"Not with a face like that!" Lenora shivered. "It was a man—or an ape. It was gray and—and bushy and sort of rippled—"

"The ripples were probably in the water," Mr. Brewster commented. "The man must have looked over your shoulder, and you saw the reflection of his face beside you."

"I didn't hear anyone behind me," Lenora returned.

"He could have been up in that tree," Beverly said thoughtfully. "It hangs low over the water, and if he parted the leaves to look down—"

"That must be the explanation," Larry nodded. "When we were after him a few minutes ago, he must have climbed the tree to escape us. That is how he disappeared so quickly."

"Let's get out of here," Lenora urged. "I don't want to see any more of him."

"Your screams probably frightened him as much as he frightened you," Beverly laughed. "I wonder who he was."

They mounted their horses and rode upstream. The hills beckoned in the distance and the trails grew less frequent and more overgrown by vines and underbrush.

Suddenly they came upon a clearing where a rough wagon road had been cut through the mass of trees to the edge of the creek. In the clearing stood a gleaming, steel-gray trailer. The door and windows were closed and curtained, but the lingering odor of smoke and bacon led them to believe someone had recently been cooking.

"This is certainly a modern touch for such a forsaken spot," Lenora commented. "Who would expect to find anyone living in a trailer way out here?"

"Hello, in there!" Mr. Brewster called loudly.

There was no response to his hail.

"He must have taken the car that towed the trailer here, and gone to town," Larry commented.

"I wonder who would take the trouble to pull that big thing all the way up here?" Lenora continued. "He must certainly want to get away from it all."

"Perhaps we'll see him another time," Mr. Brewster commented. "Let's be on our way."

They left the little stream behind and went overland until they came to a small cabin situated among a group of trees. A bearskin was spread to dry, and a bearded old man sat on the doorstep meticulously cleaning a rifle.

"Mr. Brewster!" He rose when the man from New York dismounted. "Back so soon, are ye?"

"Sooner than I expected, Ben," Mr. Brewster acknowledged, and introduced his companions. "Has Mike been back within the past few days?" he asked.

"Nope, haven't seen that young feller since the day he finished his map makin'."

"I thought he might have come back to see you," Mr. Brewster continued.

"Nope," Ben repeated. "There was another feller askin' about him, too," he added.

"There was?" Mr. Brewster was surprised. "When?"

"This mornin'," Ben answered. "He rode up on a big white horse. Said he knew Mike was comin' out here. He was a stranger to me. I never saw him before and I didn't like him. One of them city fellers," he added contemptuously.

"Aren't we all?" Lenora murmured with a smile.

Ben chuckled.

"Yes'm, but some I can take to and some I can't—if you know what I mean."

"How about a drink of water, Ben, before we start back?" Mr. Brewster asked.

"If you just want to look in the cabin to see if Mike is hidin' in there, go ahead." Ben gestured over his shoulder. "You know where the water is, too."

While the others went to quench their thirst, Beverly lingered to talk to the old westerner.

"If you see Mike, will you tell him we are in Red Camp?" she asked.

"Do you reckon he'll be glad to hear that?" Ben returned with a shrewd glance.

"Mike is in trouble back east," Beverly said in a low voice. "We came all the way out here to help him. I think he will be glad to know."

"Then I'll tell him," Ben answered.

That was all the assurance she could get out of him.

"You must have heard about us being in Red Camp," Beverly continued. "Word of strangers travels fast."

"Mebbe," he grunted.

"You must have decided to look us over, too," she continued with a smile. "You were the one spying on us a while ago, weren't you?" she asked softly. "You really frightened my friend."

"Why do you think it was me?"

"You weren't exactly surprised when we rode up.

In fact, it looked as if you were waiting for us."

"She sure can holler," he said, chuckling. "You're riding Mike's horse," he added. "She is a smart little filly."

"She is a beauty," Beverly agreed.

Lady was a gentle animal with keen intelligence. She seemed to sense her rider's intentions even before Beverly signaled. It made riding a pleasure, and Beverly was not as tired as she had expected to be after her first day in the saddle.

"Mike thought a lot of Lady," Ben continued.

"So I understand," Beverly nodded.

"Did you think he might want her and come for her when he gets here?" Ben asked.

"I did."

Ben grinned.

"You're smart, too. If you're on Mike's side in his trouble, I guess he *will* be glad to see you."

"Then we're friends?" Beverly asked.

"I'm Mike's friend first," Ben said noncommittally.

The others emerged from the little cabin and joined them, and there was no opportunity for further talk with the old man.

"It will soon be dark," Mr. Brewster observed as they remounted. "We better be getting back to the ranch. I am not too familiar with this country, and after dark it would be easy to get lost."

They waved good-bye to Ben and took to the trail single file.

"What do you make of the other man looking for Mike?" Beverly asked of Larry, who rode behind her.

"I can't imagine who it is," Larry said.

"Perhaps it is the Law," Lenora offered from up ahead. "Word does get around, you know."

"He might be Mike's confederate," Mr. Brewster called back.

"A confederate would know where Mike is," Lenora pointed out. "We will probably suspect every man on a white horse. Every easterner, that is."

"I thought we were the only strangers in Red Camp," commented Larry. "Another one shouldn't be hard to find."

They left the horses at the ranch and drove into town. Beverly found a letter from Shirley waiting for her, and she read it while they changed clothes and freshened up in their room.

"Hurrah!" Beverly exclaimed, looking up from the letter. "Listen to this, Lenora. Shirley says, 'You will be happy to know that Betsy has departed, bag and baggage. When I returned to the apartment, the very day you left, I found a note saying that Betsy had found a job and an apartment and taken both without delay. She promised to come and see us when you return.'"

"She needn't hurry," Lenora said dryly. "For not knowing anything about the big city, she's doing all right. Do you suppose she really found a job, or do you suppose she eloped with the young man we saw her meet?"

"We probably won't know the answer to that until Betsy visits us," Beverly replied. "Ready for dinner?"

"Since the Golden Nugget is the only restaurant in town, it's lucky for us they serve good food," Lenora declared, following her friend down the stairs to the lobby. "I'm so hungry I could eat a rattlesnake."

"Very tasty it is, too," Mr. Brewster told her, smiling, as he and Larry joined them in time to overhear the blonde girl's last remark.

Now that they were beginning to know Mr. Brewster better, and he them, they found he had a pleasant personality, ready to joke and laugh at Lenora's quips, or tell them interesting tales of his mining exploits. He had had a long and varied career with many adventures.

"Will you girls go ahead to the Golden Nugget and wait for us?" Larry asked. "Mr. Brewster wants to check our supplies. We'll join you in a few minutes."

Larry and Mr. Brewster entered the general store where the proprietor had gathered together the items Mr. Brewster had ordered for their camping trip.

Beverly and Lenora, meanwhile, entered the restaurant and sat down at a table. While they waited they studied a map of their proposed route which Mr. Brewster had given them.

They noticed a young man, stocky and dark complexioned, enter and sit down at a near-by table. He sipped a cup of coffee while he studied the girls. At last Lenora could stand it no longer.

"What *is* he staring at?" she whispered.

"Us," Beverly chuckled.

"That's obvious," Lenora retorted, "but why? Have you ever seen him before?"

"No. Pete—" Beverly beckoned to the proprietor. "Who is the young man at the table by the door?"

Pete looked over his shoulder and shrugged.

"I never saw him before. He must be just driving through town."

Pete went back to his work in the kitchen and the girls turned back to studying their map, but they could not concentrate. They felt the stranger's eyes boring into them and were aware of his listening ears every time they uttered a word.

"Stranger," muttered Lenora. "I wonder if he has a white horse?"

"Precisely what I was wondering," Beverly said.

"He's leaving," Lenora said urgently. "We'll never know if he has a white horse unless—"

"Yes?" Beverly said.

"We have to wait for Larry and Mr. Brewster." Lenora sighed in disappointment.

Beverly rose and hurried to the kitchen door.

"Pete, please tell Mr. Brewster we will be back in a few minutes," she directed, and rejoined Lenora.

Together the girls hurried to the door in the wake of the stranger.

It was dark now, and only two feeble street lamps and the glow from the lighted windows of the buildings illumined the main street. Neither Larry nor Mr. Brewster was in sight.

The young stranger hurried toward a car parked in front of the hotel. He got in, and a moment later the car roared past them on its way out of town.

"It certainly isn't a white horse," Lenora commented.

"There was another man in the car," Beverly said, "and a girl, too. I wonder who they are and where they are going. It is a strange route for tourists to be taking. It isn't the tourist season, either."

"The car we rented to drive to the ranch is still standing there," Lenora pointed out. "Let's follow them and see if they stop near town."

Beverly might have refused except for the fact that the young man obviously had been more than casually interested in them. Why had he watched them so intently and tried so hard to hear what they were discussing? Did he know why they were here in Red Camp, and was it possible he knew something about Mike?

"We don't have to keep on if we see they are going too far," Beverly said as she got behind the wheel of the rented automobile and Lenora climbed in beside her.

"Hurry or we'll lose them," Lenora urged.

"In the traffic?" Beverly asked laughingly.

Lenora laughed, too, because there was no other car stirring in the streets. The taillight of the car they wanted to follow glowed in the distance like a beckoning signal as Beverly sent their own car along the narrow, dusty road.

"They are going to know they are being followed," Lenora pointed out. "They'll see our headlights. Is that good?"

"We wouldn't dare drive this road without lights," Beverly replied as the car hit a rut and they bounced about. "At least they won't know *who* is following them."

"They must be on their way to Webster," Lenora deducted as they passed a faded road marker pointing southward.

"That is about five miles," Beverly replied. "Mr. Brewster told us it is no more of a thriving metropolis than Red Camp."

"They've increased their speed," Lenora said, sitting on the edge of the seat, straining her eyes through the dusty windshield. "They must have seen us and are trying to get away."

"Why should they run?" Beverly asked.

"Yes," Lenora agreed. "That is right. Why should they? Unless—" She turned to stare at her friend in the semi-darkness. "Don't laugh, Bev, but I have a feeling that this is an important discovery for us. That man knew us—or thought he did, and he was spying on us."

"I'm not laughing," Beverly said. "I have the same feeling."

"One thing," Lenora said with satisfaction, "if this

road is too dangerous for us to drive in the dark, it is too dangerous for them, too, and we can keep that taillight in sight."

Beverly did not reply, but concentrated upon her driving. The road was narrow and full of ruts. It was hard to keep the car steady and maintain any speed.

The moon rose over the valley and its light helped make their surroundings a little more distinguishable.

"We should reach Webster in another few minutes," Beverly said. "It doesn't look as though they plan to stop."

No sooner had she uttered the words than the car ahead abruptly turned off the road to follow another trail through the trees toward the black outline of a house.

Beverly pulled off the road, stopped the motor, and turned off the lights. The girls sat in silence, listening to the faint roar of the other car. In a few minutes that stopped abruptly.

"This must be their destination," Lenora murmured. "Do you suppose we mistakenly followed some innocent ranchers to their home?"

"Come on, we'll make sure," Beverly said.

The girls climbed from the car and as silently as shadows made their way to the road the other car had followed. They moved slowly along it toward the house. It was a frame building from which the paint had long since faded. Two windows were broken and the porch pillars leaned distortedly.

They saw the parked car, but the three people had disappeared.

"Where do you suppose they went so quickly?" Lenora whispered. "They could have entered the house —but it looks abandoned."

Beverly pointed beyond the house to the huge old weatherbeaten barn. The door stood partly open and from within could be seen the faint, flickering glow of a lantern.

Wordlessly the girls started forward together. All around them was silence. Only that feeble light in the barn gave indication of other life in the wilderness.

They kept to the blackness beneath the trees and approached the barn from the rear. Like shadows they slunk along the side of the building, pausing every few feet to listen and look about them.

"They *must* be in there," Lenora whispered. "What will we do?"

"I want to have a look at them," Beverly said. "But I don't want them to see me. Why don't you go back to the car and wait for me?"

"Nothing doing!" Lenora protested firmly. "This is as much my idea as yours. I want to see them, too."

Beverly nodded and began creeping toward the partly open door. Since she and Lenora had come this far, she felt compelled to get a clear glimpse of the three people they had followed. If they were strangers going about their own personal business, she and Lenora could withdraw unseen and no harm would be done. However, she had an unexplainable doubt about the man's curiosity regarding them.

The barn door was open just enough to let a slender figure slip through. After waiting and listening on the threshold, Beverly peeped cautiously into the barn. No one was in sight. The lantern sat on the bare, earthen floor, its flickering light making dancing shadows on the empty stalls surrounding it. There was another door across the room and this, too, was open. The three people must have gone into the other room.

Beverly, with Lenora close behind her, slipped into the barn and tiptoed across the floor. She was about to peep into the other room when the barn door was slammed and bolted behind them. From somewhere came a taunting laugh.

"We're trapped!" Lenora cried.

"Remember what curiosity did to the cat?" a deep, masculine voice shouted from outside. "It can happen to you, too."

"Why should it?" Beverly called back.

"You are in danger every minute you are in Red Camp," the voice continued. "Go back to New York. We know why you came, but it won't do you any good. This is a warning. Next time we will act without warning."

"Let us out of here!" Lenora cried, pounding on the rough wooden door.

"We will give you a chance to think about what I told you," the voice said with another laugh. "When

"We're trapped!" Lenora cried

you promise to go back where you came from, you will be free to go."

"We are going to stay in Red Camp until we accomplish what we came for," Beverly said firmly.

"A few hours in the old barn will change your mind," the voice called confidently.

There was the sound of an automobile motor starting up, and the girls knew they had been left alone.

"There are probably rats and bats and all sorts of things in here," Lenora said uneasily. "What'll we do, Beverly?"

"Let's explore the other room," Beverly suggested. "There may be a way out."

Beverly picked up the lantern, and holding it before them, the girls explored the small storage room. There was another door, but it too was barred. They could see no way of escape and returned to the door by which they had first entered.

"What was that?" Beverly said suddenly. "I thought I heard something."

"Probably a rat," Lenora shivered. "Who do you suppose those three characters were?"

"People who don't want us to find Mike," Beverly said with a frown. "That man in the restaurant knew exactly how to arouse our curiosity so that we would follow him. They've locked us in here to scare us."

"Well—" Lenora glanced nervously about. "I'm scared and I admit it. It might be hours before they come back to let us out—if they ever do."

"We can't count on Larry and Mr. Brewster to find us, because they don't know where we went," Beverly mused aloud. "Lenora, I believe—wait! I heard something!"

"Not again!" Lenora groaned. "It must be a whole family of rats."

"Look—" Beverly pointed to the floor. "Someone slipped a note under the door."

Slowly Lenora reached down for the piece of paper. Holding it carefully, as if she expected it to explode in her hand, she gave it to Beverly.

"You read it. I'm afraid to."

Beverly unfolded the single sheet of paper and read:

" 'You are in danger every minute. Go home at once.' " She looked up. "It is signed, 'A Friend.' "

"A friend?" Lenora looked puzzled. "Let me see the note."

Both girls stared at the crudely printed words on the torn piece of wrapping paper. There was no way of telling who had written it.

"It might be excellent advice," Lenora sighed, "but first of all we must get out of this old barn. Why didn't our friend open the door for us? Oh, if we could only escape somehow!"

In frustration and anger she threw herself against the barn door. It yielded with such suddenness, she half stumbled, half fell out into the yard.

"He did! He did!" she exclaimed hysterically. "Our mysterious friend did unlock the door!"

"Come on!" Beverly seized Lenora's hand and together they ran to where their car was parked.

"Let's head for New York and not stop until we are safely on our doorstep!" Lenora exclaimed as Beverly started the motor.

"I'd like to," Beverly agreed, "but that wouldn't be helping Mike. Besides, now more than ever, I'm determined to stay."

"Oh, I know," Lenora sighed. "Warning a reporter is like waving a red flag at a bull."

"I am not flattered at your comparison," Beverly laughed, "but I am going to find out who tried to scare us away. I also want to learn who our mysterious friend is who unlocked the barn door."

"Yes, it would be interesting to know who he is," Lenora agreed.

"I think it will prove *very* interesting," Beverly murmured thoughtfully.

CHAPTER VIII

A Spy

As THE sun rose over the mountains and the cool mist lifted from the ground, four riders and a pack horse passed through the gates of the Double-O Ranch and headed for the foothills.

The air was cool and their jackets gave welcome warmth. They breathed deeply of the morning freshness and marveled at the clear, deep blue of the sky.

The horses trotted eagerly, as if they, too, enjoyed the early morning ride.

The four people from New York had begun their camping trek in search of the gold site and Mike. After their experience of the night before, the girls had had another difficult time convincing Mr. Brewster that they should accompany him and Larry. Mr. Brewster wanted to put them on the next train for New York, but they flatly refused to go.

"We are not going to let anyone think he scared us away," Lenora declared, and Beverly nodded in firm agreement.

Mr. Brewster gave up his arguments, but he was not happy about the girls' insistence.

The morning ride was interesting but uneventful. They accomplished more than half the planned distance for the day, and enjoyed a leisurely lunch beside a narrow stream tumbling from the foothills.

"Those mountains are farther away than they look," Lenora complained as they remounted.

"Out here, distance is deceiving," Mr. Brewster agreed. "We should reach the base of Old Hank tomorrow."

"Old Hank?" Larry asked. "That's a strange name for a mountain."

"It was named for an old prospector," Mr. Brewster explained. "For years he prospected for gold in the area around the mountain. One day he came to town and boasted that he had found a rich vein on the mountain. He went back to work his claim and has never been seen since. The mountain apparently swallowed him."

"I hope there won't be any cause to change the name to Old Lenora," the blonde girl murmured.

"It's just a story," Mr. Brewster assured her. "Probably Hank's strike wasn't as good as he at first thought, and he moved on to better diggings."

They rode on toward the purple haze of hills. Near

midafternoon they came to the crest of a small rise of ground. Among the trees stood the same trailer they had seen the day before. This time there was a car hooked to it and a man could be seen bent under the open hood.

Beverly and her friends rode up and hailed him. He turned about slowly, adjusting a pair of dark glasses as he did so. He was about six feet tall, tanned, with flaming red hair beneath a battered brown hat. The dark glasses effectually hid his eyes. When he spoke, his voice was high and unpleasant.

"Having trouble with your car?" Larry asked. "It is hard to pull such a heavy trailer over these roads."

"I haven't much farther to go," the stranger said. "I am a geologist. I want to study the rocks in the foot-hills. Are you tourists?"

"In a way," Mr. Brewster nodded. "You won't find any camp in which to get water or electricity for your house on wheels."

"I am prepared for that," the young man answered. "Would you care to have a cool drink before you go on your way?"

"Yes, thank you, we would," Lenora accepted promptly.

She slid off Red and started for the trailer.

"If you will wait here, I'll get it for you," the man volunteered hastily.

He disappeared into his house and Lenora turned in disappointment to Beverly.

"I wanted to see the inside of the trailer," she complained.

Beverly dismounted and patted Lady soothingly. The horse had begun to move restlessly. She had whinnied softly when the strange young man spoke to them, and she obviously wanted to follow him.

"What's the matter, Lady?" Beverly asked softly. "Quiet now!"

"His red hair probably scared her," Lenora whispered with a giggle. "Isn't it a horrible shade of red?"

The man reappeared with a tray on which were five glasses and a pitcher of cool lemonade.

"My name is Leahcim," he said as he handed a filled glass to Lenora.

The others introduced themselves, and he asked:

"Are you interested in rocks?"

"If you have any gold-bearing ones, we are," Lenora answered.

"You don't look like prospectors," he commented, "and it isn't exactly the tourist season."

His statement obviously called for further explanation from them, but no one made it.

"We must be going if we hope to reach our camp site before dark," Mr. Brewster declared.

They thanked the young man for the refreshment and rode off down the trail. The man closed the hood of his car, locked the door of his trailer, and slowly drove down the road in the same direction taken by Beverly and her friends.

They made camp that night near the same stream they had followed nearly all day. There was a small canvas tent for the girls, while Larry and Mr. Brewster were comfortable in sleeping bags beside the campfire.

"Bev," Lenora inquired sleepily as they lay in the darkness, "do you suppose that fellow Leahcim is the man on the white horse?"

"I doubt it," Beverly said. "Did you expect to see the horse in his trailer?"

"I hope we find Mike before anyone else does," Lenora continued drowsily. "I have a funny feeling that he is in danger—"

"If we reach the gold site tomorrow or the next day, we may see him then," Beverly said.

Lenora made no comment. She was fast asleep. Beverly lay wakeful for a long while, thinking about Mike, the strange man who was looking for him, and the red-haired man they had met today.

The odor of bacon frying wakened the girls in the morning and they stepped out of their tent to see Larry and Mr. Brewster making breakfast. The girls splashed the cool creek water on their faces and returned to camp glowing and laughing.

"Did you know Larry could cook when you decided to marry him, Bev?" Lenora inquired.

"No," Beverly laughed. "I am just discovering his hidden talent."

"Bacon and eggs are the extent of my culinary achievements," Larry assured them.

"What are we going to eat on this camping trip?" Lenora asked.

"I can flip a mean pancake," Mr. Brewster boasted, grinning. "We'll do all right."

"And gain about ten pounds," Lenora groaned.

"How far are we going to travel today?" Beverly wanted to know.

"We hope to reach the base of Old Hank," Larry told her.

"We will establish camp there and explore the foot-hills carefully," added Mr. Brewster. "It is very rough country. I hope you young ladies will be all right. Remember, I didn't—"

"We know," Lenora interrupted hastily. "You didn't want us to come along. This was our own idea. We'll manage—you'll see."

They struck camp immediately after breakfast, and rode without stopping until the sun was high in the heaven and the horses needed rest. They did not linger long over lunch, but pressed on through rugged, beautiful country until at last Old Hank rose above them.

"Somehow he doesn't seem so big now," Lenora said, gazing up at the summit. "I'm going to climb to the top of him one of these days."

"It shouldn't be too difficult for you," Mr. Brewster said. "There is a path almost to the summit. Mike and I climbed it easily. There is a sheepherder who sometimes grazes his sheep on the slopes. We'll probably meet him in a day or two."

"Where shall we camp?" Larry asked.

"There is a small stream of water around the other side," Mr. Brewster answered. "It might even have some fish in it."

This time, since the camp was to be more permanent, they put up two tents—one for the girls and one for the men.

A brief but heavy shower drove them into their tents soon after dinner, and they used it as a welcome excuse to retire early. The ride had been more tiring than any of them would admit. It had been a long, long time since the girls spent so many hours in the saddle, and little-used muscles were crying for rest.

The moon emerged from behind the clouds during the night and bathed the camp in silver light. No one was awake to notice the dark figure that stood silhouetted on Old Hank and studied their silent camp for several minutes before he slunk away into the darkness.

They rose soon after sunrise the next morning and made plans for the day while they ate breakfast.

"I am going to stay right here and rest this morning," Lenora announced before anyone else said anything. "If you ambitious people want to ride, go ahead. I am going to give Red and my saddle a rest. Maybe I'll try my hand at fishing in the creek and catch some fish for dinner."

"Larry and I planned to ride along the ridge and see if we can find the twin pines," Mr. Brewster stated.

"What about you, Bev?" Larry asked. "Do you want to come with Mr. Brewster and me?"

"No. I think I'll climb part way up Old Hank and survey the countryside," Beverly answered. "The view should be marvelous from up there."

It was agreed that they should each do as they pleased this morning, and Larry and Mr. Brewster rode off immediately after breakfast.

Beverly and Lenora washed the tin dishes and then the blonde girl brought out her camera.

"I have to put in some new film," she said. "Then I am going to find a nice comfortable seat and wait for that little groundhog to come out of his hole over there. Charlie Blaine can use a closeup of him next Groundhog Day."

Beverly laughed and started out on her walk. The sun was warm on her back as she began the climb up the side of Old Hank. The path was steep and narrow, but there were plenty of places to rest.

The ground was damp from the previous night's shower, and Beverly found herself unconsciously following a set of footprints which led along the path and out onto a ledge from which she had an unobstructed view of their camp far below. When she thought about the footprints she grew puzzled. Whoever had made them had come this way since the rain. To gain the path up the side of Old Hank, he must have had to pass their camp. The mysterious stranger had stood exactly where she now stood, and the only thing of interest to view was their camp. Someone had spied upon them without their knowledge, and it gave her a cold, apprehensive feeling. However, there was nothing to be done about it.

Old Hank was but one of the hills that ringed the little valley, and between one hill and the next, lacing them together, were stretches of rock, forest, and untilled land. Somewhere in this vicinity lay the twin pines near which Mr. Brewster and Mike had made their gold discovery. The hills kept the secret well, and it might take a long time to discover the exact spot again, unless they had the maps Mike had made— or Mike himself to help them.

Beverly decided not to go any farther, but to save climbing to the summit until Lenora was with her. She found a path down the side opposite from their camp and set out to explore some of the green forest on foot.

It was a nature lover's paradise. Tiny woodland flowers she had never seen before peeked from under the green brush. Birds strange to her twittered on branches overhead. Over it all was the heavy, hushed silence of the woods. Many of the trees were pines, and their needles blanketed the ground with a slippery green that was treacherous to her unwary feet. As she turned to go back to camp, Beverly slipped down a small incline. She landed in a heap at the bottom, one foot caught in the jaws of a rusty, abandoned hunter's trap.

CHAPTER IX

The Rescuer

It HAD all happened with such suddenness that Beverly was stunned for a moment. Then she sat up and tried to extricate her foot, but it was caught and held in such a position behind her that she could not reach it with both hands.

"This is a fine mess!" she told herself. "Why didn't you watch where you were going?"

She doubted if Lenora, in camp, would hear her if she called. She was too far away for her voice to carry that distance. Still, she must try. It was her only hope.

Beverly called for help and waited. Then she called again. Neither time was there any response. She tried to twist herself about to reach the trap, but it was impossible. To pull on it only made the rusty teeth of the trap close more tightly on her boot. She tried to slip her foot out of the boot, but it was caught above

She tried to slip her foot out of the boot

the ankle and she could not. She had visions of herself stranded here for hours—perhaps even overnight. It was not pleasant to think about. There were probably snakes and—

"I'll shout again," she told herself.

Her voice echoed back to her, but there was no other response. She called again and again. At last she began to despair of anyone finding her. She tried to tell herself Mr. Brewster and Larry would come in search of her. But she could not expect even that for hours. In the meantime her foot was becoming numb and her leg ached from the awkward position.

Once more she called aloud. What was that? It sounded like the snap of a twig. There was a stirring in the underbrush. Was it an animal? Beverly held her breath and waited, her heart pounding in her ears.

"You *are* in difficulty, aren't you?" a masculine voice said.

The bushes parted and the geologist, Leahcim, stepped into view.

"I heard you calling, but I couldn't locate you immediately," he explained. "I'll have you free in a minute."

He bent over the trap, his gloved hands straining at the steel teeth.

"It is stiff with rust," he grunted and sat back on his heels to consider the situation.

"It is a little heavy to wear as an anklet for very long," Beverly commented with a faint smile.

"That's the spirit!" he commended. "I'll get you out of it, don't worry. Are you in any pain?"

"My foot is numb," Beverly answered. "I don't think it has done any permanent damage yet."

"Your heavy boot has kept the teeth from reaching the skin," he agreed. "Can you hold your leg a little higher while I try to force this stick between the jaws?"

"I'll try," Beverly nodded. "It certainly is fortunate for me that you happened along."

"Yes, isn't it?" he agreed. "Where are your friends?"

"Each of us went different ways today," she said. "Are you succeeding with the stick?"

"A few more minutes will do the trick," he said, bending to his task with determination. "You shouldn't go wandering about alone in country strange to you," he declared. "It's too easy to get lost."

Beverly watched him as he worked over the stubborn trap. She decided he was younger than his red hair and battered hat made him look. She could not tell what color his eyes were or see their expression behind the dark glasses. Even his hands, which might have revealed more of his character, were hidden with gloves. Definitely, there was something odd about him.

"Do you have a white horse?" she asked impulsively.

"I have a trailer," he answered. "What would I do with a horse? Here it comes!"

With a final effort, he had pressed the jaws of the trap apart and Beverly pulled her boot free. She scrambled to her feet and immediately would have fallen if he had not caught her. The numb foot would not bear her weight at once.

"We must get the circulation back," he said. "Sit down."

Beverly collapsed onto a log and he carefully removed her boot. With hands that were surprisingly gentle, he massaged her foot and ankle.

"I can do that," Beverly said, a bit embarrassed, pulling away.

"Sit still, Beverly!" he exclaimed and resumed his rubbing.

"How did you know my name?" she asked.

His head was bent and the broad brim of his hat hid his face from view.

"You told me when you introduced yourself the other day," he said. "Sorry if I was too informal." He put her foot on the ground. "Try to stand."

Slowly Beverly brought her weight to bear on the injured foot.

"It will be all right in a few moments," she assured him.

"Can you find your way back to your camp?" he asked.

"Yes, I think so," she replied. "I can't ever thank you enough."

"Forget it," he said crisply. "Good day, Miss Gray."

He strode away and was swallowed up in the underbrush, leaving her staring after him more mystified than ever.

There definitely was something strange about him, she thought again. One minute he had called her Beverly and the next, apologized for being informal. He had helped her all he could and then rushed away without being thanked.

Beverly began her walk back to camp. She went carefully because of her foot, and slowly because she was preoccupied with thoughts of Leahcim.

It was possible that a geologist would come here to study the rock formations. But was that all he had come here for, or was he, too, after gold?

Both times that she had met Leahcim, she had the feeling that he was studying her. She could feel his eyes penetrating through the dark glasses.

And she had the strongest feeling that she had met him before. The lift of his head, the wide smile—when he did smile, which wasn't often—and the width of his shoulders when he bent over the trap on her foot. Now that she thought of it, they were just like—

She had come to the edge of their camp site when she had the sudden thought. Now she stood still, head bent in concentration.

"Behold, the gal who walks in her sleep!" Lenora's voice penetrated through the haze of Beverly's thoughts. "You *must* be sleeping. I said 'hello' at least three times. We had begun to think you didn't want any lunch."

"Where've you been, Bev?" Larry added.

"I've had an adventure," she said, smiling, joining

her three friends. "Feed me and I'll tell you all about it."

"So the geologist came to your rescue," Lenora exclaimed when Beverly had finished her story.

"We saw his trailer parked downstream," Mr. Brewster volunteered. "He is a peculiar chap."

"How do you mean?" Beverly asked.

"Oh—coming out here alone in that big trailer," Mr. Brewster said vaguely. "It just strikes me as a bit queer."

"At any rate, we're grateful to him for helping Beverly," Larry said. "Are you sure your foot is all right now?"

"Oh, yes," Beverly assured him. "You can see the marks of the trap on my boot, but the leather is not cut through."

"You better not go walking off alone any more," Larry counseled.

"No," Beverly agreed. "I'm going to ride Lady this afternoon. Did you find the twin pines this morning?"

"No. We're going to try a different direction after lunch." Mr. Brewster frowned. "I'm sure they are in this vicinity somewhere."

"If Mike were only here," Lenora sighed.

"If Mike had been as honest as I thought he was, *we* wouldn't be here," Mr. Brewster said in irritation.

Talking about Mike occupied them until the two men rode off to the north. Beverly on Lady went in the opposite direction. She carefully followed the stream, not relishing the idea of getting lost. Lady picked her way carefully and Beverly did not urge her to haste. She had learned to trust her horse and depend upon her to find firm footing in difficult spots.

At last, through the trees, she saw the sun glinting on the silver trailer. She halted Lady and studied the house on wheels without revealing herself. The door was open, but apparently Leahcim was not there.

Beverly dismounted and tied her horse to a tree. Then she approached the trailer on foot. She called the geologist's name aloud, but Leahcim did not reply. She went to the door of the trailer and peered inside. The trailer looked cozy and inviting. She knocked on the open door and then stepped inside. It was furnished simply but comfortably. The center of the trailer was a kitchen, complete with refrigerator, stove, and cabinets. At the far end she could see a bedroom. Where she stood was the dining and lounging area.

There was a small television set, bookshelves under the windows at the end, a dropleaf table, and two comfortable chairs as well as a small couch. There were a number of books on mining and engineering, as well as a group of popular magazines. The man who was here to study rocks evidently did not believe in bringing samples of his work home with him. There was not a rock to be seen.

Beverly decided to investigate further. She peeped into the bedroom, noted the carefully arranged closet, and went on with her search. In the cabinet in the tiny bathroom she found what she was looking for, and she smiled to herself with satisfaction.

At that moment she heard hoofbeats outside. Had Leahcim returned—on horseback?

She went to the door which she had carefully shut behind her when she entered the trailer, and now she locked it. Then she cautiously peeped out a window. A man, not Leahcim, was sitting on a big white horse, looking at the trailer.

CHAPTER X

Leahcim

THE rider sat thoughtfully considering the trailer in silence for several moments.

"Hello in there!" he called at last.

When there was no response, the man dismounted and strode toward the trailer. He was young and heavyset, with a swarthy complexion. It was the same man whom the girls had followed from the restaurant in Red Camp. Beverly recognized him with inward excitement.

"Did you want to see me?" Leahcim suddenly strode out of the surrounding trees.

Had the geologist been concealed in the brush all this time? Had he seen her, Beverly, enter his trailer?

"Have you been camped here very long?" the stranger asked.

"A day or two," Leahcim answered cautiously. "Why?"

"Perhaps you can help me," the man continued. "I am looking for a young man—a mining engineer. He is camped somewhere around here. He is about your height, but with black hair and eyes. His name is Mc-Kay—Michael McKay."

"There is a party of campers about a mile from here," Leahcim answered. "Perhaps he is one of them."

"No, he isn't," the man replied.

Beverly realized as he spoke that this must be the owner of the footprints she had seen on Old Hank. He must have been the one who spied on their camp the previous night. That was why he could be so positive now that Mike was not with them.

"When he was here a few weeks ago, he had a favorite horse. That's it, tethered over there."

"Lady?" Leahcim said in surprise. "She comes from the Double-O Ranch. Anyone can hire her."

"Did you?"

Leahcim pushed his battered hat back on his flaming red hair and considered the man on the white horse carefully through his dark glasses. His high voice was irritable when he spoke.

"It seems to me you are asking a lot of questions. I don't like nosy people. I'd be much obliged if you would leave my camp."

"Is it your horse?" the man repeated.

"No, it isn't," Leahcim returned.

The stranger mounted his white stallion and sat looking down at Leahcim for a thoughtful moment. Then he wheeled his horse and trotted away.

Not until the hoofbeats died away in the distance did Leahcim move. He came toward the trailer door and Beverly hurriedly unlocked it.

Leahcim pulled open the door and stepped inside. Beverly was seated on the divan with a magazine in her hand.

"Hi!" she said pleasantly.

"What are you doing here?" he demanded.

"Snooping," she said frankly. "I must say you did a good job."

"A good job of what?"

"Of fooling us," she continued. "That first day none of us suspected."

"Suspected what?" He persisted in pretending not to know what she meant.

"Oh, Mike!" she exclaimed. "I know you dyed your hair. I found the dye in the cabinet in the bathroom. I think you are hiding here to catch the real thief. We want to help you."

He flung his battered hat to the table and collapsed into a chair opposite her.

"Beverly Gray, reporter, gets another scoop," he announced, grinning sheepishly.

"Won't Lenora and Larry be surprised!" Beverly chuckled. "I don't believe they suspect a thing."

"And they mustn't," he said hurriedly. "This is your

surprise, Bev. Yours and mine! I don't want anyone else to know yet. Promise?"

"But why?" she asked.

"Because when I face Mr. Brewster, I want to have the real thief with me," Mike said grimly.

"Tell me what really happened that night in Mr. Brewster's library," Beverly said. "Do you know who the real thief is?"

"The story starts much farther back than that," Mike told her. "It starts in Red Camp the night John Brewster was flown east and I stayed behind. I worked in my hotel room until late, compiling some of the data for the maps and charts we would need. When I went to bed I couldn't fall asleep right away. I lay thinking of all the things the gold strike could mean—to me personally as well as to the company. Today there are discoveries which can be more valuable than gold, but just the word 'gold' has a magic in it that arouses one's dreams. I had a good job and it looked like a promising future. I could ask Lenora to marry me.

"I suppose by this time I was half asleep, but suddenly I was aware of someone in my room. He had climbed through the window and was making off with my briefcase of notes and charts. I leaped on him. We struggled and the hassle woke everyone else in the hotel. When someone pounded on my door he took off through the window again, but in the moonlight I got a good look at his face. I know I would recognize him again.

"The next day I moved out to old Ben's cabin. I finished my work there."

"Did you ever see the intruder again?" Beverly asked.

"I'm coming to that," Mike replied. "I flew east and took all the papers to John. It was late in the day when I arrived at his house, and he invited me to stay for dinner. He had his secretary and her brother to dinner also. I had met her before, of course, in the office. She had always been very nice to me. In fact, when I took her to lunch once or twice, I told her about you girls and Lenora being in New York. I thought you might like to meet her.

"We played bridge after dinner. Once Miss Jones went to get a handkerchief from her coat, and once her brother went out to telephone."

"That much agrees with what Mr. Brewster told us," Beverly nodded. "Go on."

"I excused myself early, because I was tired. They were having a heated discussion over something and I said I would let myself out. On the way I decided to telephone Lenora and went into the library to use the telephone. I saw at once the desk had been broken into, and then I pulled the prize blooper of them all. I picked up the broken drawer instead of letting it strictly alone."

"That accounts for your fingerprints," Beverly said. "Oh, Mike!"

"Yes," he said gloomily, "and after all the mystery stories I've read! I know better than to touch anything at the scene of the crime—or I always thought I did. That night I was so surprised and shocked at what had happened, I didn't really realize what I did. I knew at once who must have taken them, but I knew no one would believe me without proof. When I heard some-one coming toward the library I hid, to see what would happen.

"John discovered the theft and called Inspector Travers. He must have told you the rest."

"Yes," Beverly said, "but why won't you let us help you, Mike? If you know who has the plans—"

"He has gone undercover, too," Mike said. "He is hiding from John Brewster while he hunts for me."

"But why?" Beverly persisted. "If he has all the papers, why is he after you? Isn't it enough that you are the suspected thief?"

"The plans aren't any good to him." Mike grinned with satisfaction. "You see, after that night in the hotel when I learned someone else wanted the maps and information, I charted everything in code. I didn't tell John that—I didn't have a chance the day I arrived. I intended to tell him later when we went over the plans together. As it is now—well, to use the plans, the thief has to find me and make me give him the code."

"I hope you have the code in a safe place," Beverly sighed.

"I do," Mike assured her.

"Have you seen this man since you have been out here?"

"Yes, once," Mike nodded. "It was the night you were trapped in the barn."

"If you know the real thief, why don't you have him arrested?" Beverly demanded.

"He disappears like a phantom." Mike said, frowning. "I want to learn where he is living, and then I want to bring him and John Brewster face to face."

"Don't waste time on dramatics," Beverly said urgently. "Get the law after him as soon as possible."

"Who would believe me?" Mike demanded. "I have been branded the thief, remember? This man is a respected member of society, a friend of John Brewster. He would deny my accusation, and who would believe me? I've got to have proof."

"That means you must recover the stolen papers."

"Exactly!" Mike agreed. "I want to get the thief and his accomplices all at once."

"But he is hunting you in the meantime," Beverly said. "It isn't safe for you, Mike—"

"He doesn't suspect Leahcim." Mike smiled. "Therein lies my safety—and yours. Why didn't you follow the advice I gave you the other night?"

"You were our unseen friend!" Beverly exclaimed. "I should have suspected it. That man on the white horse just now—he was the one we followed from the restaurant. How did you know we were in the barn?"

"I overheard him and the girl plotting to frighten you into going home," Mike answered. "You should have gone."

"We want to help you," Beverly returned. "How can we best do that?"

"Right at the moment there is nothing anyone can do," he replied. "If I need you I'll send you word, but I don't want to do that. As I said—they don't realize who Leahcim is. They are trying to locate the gold while they look for Michael McKay. When they see Leahcim they think I am only interested in rocks. I spend a lot of my time near the old deserted mines, and sooner or later I'll find the man and the proof I want."

"But, Mike—" Beverly protested.

"If they knew who I was and that you were trying to help me, neither of us would be safe. Don't you see? That is why you must keep my secret. Don't come here again. Don't try to contact me—"

"You can't insist on that," Beverly said firmly. "I'll keep your secret only if you will let me work with you in capturing the real thief."

"Now Beverly—" Mike began.

"Your secret will be safe with me," she assured him. "It will be a big surprise for the others, and I don't know how I'll ever keep from telling them, but I will. Please let me help."

"It's against my better judgment, but all right," he sighed. "Tell me, Miss Gray," he resumed in the high voice of the geologist, "what are your plans for tomorrow?"

Beverly, too, had heard the hoofbeats outside and entered at once into the spirit of his disguise.

"I thought I might go for a ride in the morning," she said. "Perhaps we could meet for another talk—"

"That would be cozy!" an angry voice said from the open doorway.

"Larry!" Beverly exclaimed in amazement.

"Come in," Leahcim invited cordially.

"No, thank you!" Larry said coldly. "When you did not return to camp, Beverly, we were afraid you might have had another accident, so I came to look for you. I am sorry if I am intruding!" He turned on his heel and strode away to his horse.

"He's jealous!" Beverly whispered incredulously. "Mike—"

"Leahcim!" the young man corrected. "Remember your promise, Bev. You are not to tell anyone who I really am!"

"But if Larry—"

"You promised not to tell anyone!" Leahcim repeated firmly.

Beverly stared at him in dismay. Keeping Mike's secret promised complications of which she had not dreamed.

CHAPTER XI

Turning the Tables

"LARRY! Larry, wait!"

Beverly ran to Lady, caught up the reins, and rode after her fiancé.

"Larry, what's the matter?" she asked breathlessly when she rode up beside him.

"We were worried about you," he said bluntly, "and all the while you were sitting there chatting with a strange man."

"He isn't a stranger—" Beverly flung out and checked herself. "I mean, we all met him the other day, and this morning he rescued me—"

"I suppose he was telling you all about rocks," Larry interrupted.

"You might learn something, too, if you became better acquainted with him," she said hotly, stung by his jealous tone.

"*I'm* out here on business," Larry said stiffly.

"What has gotten into you?" she demanded. "Surely you're not jealous just because I stopped to talk—"

"I'm not jealous!" Larry denied. "You can talk to him all you like, but I thought we came out here to find Mike. Or have you decided to study rocks instead?"

Beverly's own anger was rising to meet his. In another moment they would be quarreling—and it was silly to quarrel when all the time Leahcim *was* Mike. If only she could explain it all to Larry, but she had promised Mike to keep his secret.

Beverly and Larry rode the rest of the way back to camp in silence. There he helped her to dismount.

"I'm sorry I spoke as I did, Beverly," he said slowly.

"I'm sorry I made you worry about me," she replied with a smile. "I honestly didn't realize how long I had been gone. Did you find the twin pines?"

"No, we didn't," Mr. Brewster replied, joining them, "but I am sure they are in this section. This is the Barker land and it was on this property we discovered it. Of course, the Barkers owned miles of this stuff—" He gestured around them with a sweep of his hand.

"There are so many gullies and mountain passes that it'll take time to explore them all," Larry added.

"Did you ask old Ben if he knows where they are?" Beverly suggested.

"We met him this morning, but he couldn't help us," Mr. Brewster replied.

"Do you think Mike is already at the gold site?" asked Lenora, who had come out to meet them.

"Probably," Mr. Brewster said with a frown.

"He can't dig the gold out alone," Larry said, "and there hasn't been time for any big-scale operation."

"You sound now as though *you* believe Mike wants the gold for himself," Lenora said accusingly.

"No," Larry denied, "but I do think he will turn up at the gold site."

"Suppose he has been there and gone before we find it?" Lenora persisted. "What then?"

"Then we will wait until someone comes to dig the gold," Mr. Brewster said grimly. "How about having dinner?"

"Did you know someone was spying on our camp last night?" Beverly asked as they relaxed later by the fire.

She told them of the footprints she had seen that morning.

"Mike!" Mr. Brewster guessed immediately.

"But Mike knows we are his friends," Lenora protested. "He doesn't have to spy on us. He could walk right down and join us."

"He could, but he knows I'd take him into town to the sheriff," Mr. Brewster said.

"I don't think it was Mike," Beverly put in.

"Then who was it?" Lenora wanted to know.

"I saw the man on the white horse today," Beverly said.

"You *did* have a busy day, didn't you?" Larry remarked, smiling. "Is he a friend of the geologist?"

"He stopped at the trailer to ask about Mike," Beverly replied.

"What does he look like?" Lenora demanded. "Tell us everything!"

"It was the same man who came into the restaurant in Red Camp," Beverly replied.

"The one we followed?" Lenora asked in surprise. "What did he do when he saw you?"

"He didn't see me," Beverly said. "I stayed in the trailer. He saw Lady, but he didn't know who was riding her."

Lenora glanced over her shoulder at the black shadows surrounding the friendly glow of the fire.

"I don't like to think there are unseen eyes and ears watching and listening to us," she shivered. "He could be watching us from up there on the mountain. I think I'll go to bed and pull the blanket up over my head."

"I agree with the going-to-bed part," Beverly said, getting up. "There is nothing we can do tonight anyway."

Good nights were said and the girls retired to their tent. In the glow of a kerosene lantern Lenora brushed her blonde hair thoughtfully.

"You know, Bev, sometimes I think we were foolish to come out here."

"Why?"

"I'll bet Mike is in New York laughing at us this very minute."

"I'll bet he isn't in New York and he isn't laughing," Beverly replied, pulling off her boots.

"Then you believe, as Larry and Mr. Brewster do, that we will find him here?" Lenora said.

"I certainly do," Beverly declared, and wished she could tell her friend more.

"I wish I were as confident as you are," Lenora sighed drowsily.

Beverly lay awake long after the others were quiet. The night noises were strange and exciting. A horse whinnied and an owl hooted dismally. She wondered if the man on the white horse were spying on them again.

She must find a way to talk to Mike tomorrow. There were so many more questions she wanted to ask him. What was the name of the real thief? Why didn't Mike tell Mr. Brewster all about it and take the chance that his employer would believe him? She could understand how his first panic had sent him into hiding, but now—

Still, Mr. Brewster could be a very difficult person sometimes. And finding Mike's fingerprints on the desk had convicted him in Mr. Brewster's mind.

It had been a master stroke to put the maps and charts in code and so make them worthless to a thief. It would most certainly draw the thief into action. The only trouble was, Mike had made himself the bait. It was not a safe or enviable position.

The next morning was cloudy and cool. Larry and Mr. Brewster rode off early to investigate an abandoned mine they had passed the previous day. Beverly and Lenora declared their intention of climbing to the top of Old Hank to view the countryside and Lenora prepared herself with her camera and Shirley's powerful binoculars.

"I always thought of this country as being nothing but one ranch after another," the blonde girl said as they made their first stop, halfway to the summit.

"Farther south, it may be," Beverly agreed, "but there isn't much grazing land around here. To the north of us are more mountains and even ice caps."

"Glacier Park," Lenora nodded. "It is beautiful there —lakes and mountains and snow in July, on the mountain tops, that is."

"And Blackfeet Indians," Beverly added with a smile. "May I borrow your binoculars a moment?"

While Lenora tried to capture the view of the valley behind them with her camera, Beverly scanned the scene through the powerful glasses.

She located the trailer but could see no sign of life around it. She wondered what Mike was doing.

Sweeping the binoculars over the scene, she halted and focused the glasses more sharply. A white horse! The animal was clearly visible against the green of the underbrush. His rider was a man, but his back was toward her. He seemed to be alone, riding a course parallel to the foothills.

Beverly handed the glasses to Lenora and indicated the rider.

"I see him! I see him!" Lenora cried.

She studied the figure for several minutes. "I wish he would turn around so I could see his face."

"He must be living somewhere close by," Beverly said. "Let's go to the top and then take another look around."

"Okay, let's," Lenora agreed eagerly. "From up there we might even be able to see the rocks Mike called twin pines."

The last half of the climb to the summit was more difficult. There was no established trail, and loose stones made footing uncertain. However, once they had reached the summit, they felt it was worth all their effort.

The valley lay behind them green and peaceful, with silver threads of water like ribbons joining field and forest. Before them the mountains rose in haughty grandeur, their peaks lost in fleecy white puffs of clouds.

"It is breathtaking," Beverly sighed, viewing the splendor before them.

"But doesn't it make you feel *little* and insignificant?" Lenora whispered, awe-stricken. "I thought Old Hank was high, but now—"

"Old Hank is a mere ant hill," Beverly chuckled. "May I have the glasses?"

"Here—" Lenora handed the binoculars to her companion while she gazed in reverent silence at the world around her.

"For once I'm speechless," she declared.

"It took mountains to achieve that," Beverly teased.

"Now I know what the song means by 'purple mountain majesties,'" Lenora said after a moment. She brought her thoughts back to their mission. "Do you see the white horse any more?"

"Yes," Beverly said. "He is still moving in the same direction, and I think—yes—it is! Look, Lenora, there is a cabin on that other hill. That must be where he is living."

Lenora studied the scene before she spoke.

"It isn't so far from our camp. Do you think we could find it?"

"We could try," Beverly said at once.

"If he is looking for Mike, we might learn something by watching him. We could turn the tables and spy on him for a change."

"Remember the barn," Beverly reminded her, smiling. "Are you sure you want to do it?"

"This time we won't let him know we are spying," Lenora said. "Let's investigate the cabin this afternoon."

Beverly agreed and the girls began their descent of Old Hank.

Once in camp they made lunch and waited for Larry and Mr. Brewster to return. They waited more than an hour and then Lenora was too impatient to wait longer. They left a note for Larry, saddled their horses, and rode off in the direction in which they had seen the man on the white horse traveling that morning.

On the way, they passed the trailer, but "Leahcim" was not visible and they did not linger. They rode on along a narrow, almost hidden, foot trail. When the path began to climb they knew they were getting close to the cabin they had seen, and their eagerness deepened.

They came to the clearing where the cabin was located, and after watching from the protection of the surrounding trees, they decided the place was empty.

"Maybe he doesn't live here after all," Lenora said with a frown. "It doesn't look like much of a place," she added, considering the tiny house.

"I'm going to take a look inside," Beverly said and dismounted.

"Not without me," Lenora cried, following closely behind her friend.

Together they pushed open the small cabin door and stepped inside.

A table and several chairs stood before the fireplace. There were several cooking utensils, a jug of water, as well as some dirty dishes, on the table. A rifle stood against the wall beside a door leading to a room beyond. There were also three knapsacks piled on the floor beside two wooden bunk beds.

"Someone is living here," Lenora observed. "I don't like it, Bev. Let's get out of here."

"In a moment," Beverly nodded. "I wonder where that other door leads."

"Suppose the man with the white horse comes and finds us here?" Lenora continued with a shiver. "He won't like us breaking into his house."

"We didn't break in," Beverly corrected. "The door was unlocked."

She moved across the room and tried the other door. It swung open easily and she stood on the threshold looking around. "Oh!" Beverly exclaimed.

"What is it?" Lenora came to peer over her friend's shoulder.

"The girl who was in the car must be living here, too," Beverly said.

There was a dress lying on the narrow cot bed, a girl's coat on the one chair, and shoes beside the leather suitcase.

"I wish we could see what she looks like," Beverly added. "It was too dark that night."

"I'd like to know what she looks like, too," Lenora agreed, "but I'd rather not be here when they get back," she finished uneasily.

Beverly closed the door and the girls turned back to the larger room.

"I wonder where they came from and why," Beverly murmured.

"After what the man said that night at the barn, we know they are hunting for Mike," Lenora pointed out.

"But the girl—" Beverly murmured.

A brief flash of unhappiness crossed Lenora's face.

"Yes, the girl! I wonder why she is looking for him?"

Lenora immediately had thought of a romantic at-
tachment, but Beverly had other ideas.

"I don't know why," Beverly said, "but I don't believe
we should wait here to ask her. Let's go."

"A very wise decision," a voice said behind the girls.
"I only hope it isn't too late."

CHAPTER XII

The Mine

LEAHCIM stood in the doorway of the cabin. His battered hat was pushed down on his red hair and, as usual, his dark glasses hid his eyes.

Beverly thought absently how well Mike's experience in college dramatics was serving him in his present disguise.

Leahcim motioned to them and spoke in his unpleasant, high voice.

"You better leave at once. The man with the white horse is coming up the path now."

"Uh-oh!" Lenora exclaimed. "Is there time for us to get away?"

"If you hurry," Leahcim said. "Continue up the path about a hundred yards. There you will see another path leading east. Follow it for another hundred yards and then you can descend unseen."

"Are you going to wait here for him?" Beverly asked when the girls were mounted.

"Oh, no," Leahcim answered. "I'll disappear, too. Don't worry about me. Get away while you can."

The girls rode off swiftly. Beverly glanced back before they disappeared among the trees, but Leahcim had already vanished from the clearing. She wondered how he had known they were in the cabin. He must have been watching the place, just as he had been watching the old barn several nights ago.

The girls easily found the path to descend and they made their way back to their camp without incident. There Larry and Mr. Brewster were waiting impatiently for them.

"Did you find the twin pines?" Lenora asked eagerly.

"No," Larry said, "but we have news."

"What?" the blonde girl demanded anxiously. "Have you seen Mike?"

"We were talking to a man who was riding to Red Camp from Wilkins, and he told us there is a young man answering Mike's description camped just over the next ridge. We thought you would want to go with us to investigate."

"Of course we do," Lenora said. "Won't Mike be surprised when we drop in on him?"

"Suppose it isn't Mike?" Beverly said slowly.

"The general description fits him," Mr. Brewster told her. "But we will make sure."

"But—"

Beverly broke off helplessly. She *knew* it wasn't Mike, but how could she tell them without breaking her promise?

"If you don't mind, I'll wait for you here," Beverly said.

"Beverly!" Lenora exclaimed in surprise.

"I thought you were as anxious to find Mike as we are," added Larry.

"Yes, Miss Gray." Mr. Brewster looked at Beverly sharply. "Don't you feel well? Is something wrong?"

"No," Beverly assured them. "Nothing is wrong."

"What would you do while we are gone?" Larry asked. "It may take several hours. Won't you be lonely? Or do you plan to go and learn more about the local rocks?"

She had planned to go and see Mike, but after Larry's remark she knew it would not be wise. Her fiancé still felt hurt over the needless anxiety she had caused him yesterday.

"Very well," Beverly sighed. "I'll go with you."

They mounted their horses and rode off swiftly, everyone but Beverly anxious to see the young man answering Mike's description. They took a diagonal northern course from Old Hank, through a narrow, rocky gorge cut by a long-vanished stream. They waved to the sheepherder on the hillside, but they did not stop to chat with him.

"I can't wait to see Mike's face when we surprise him," Lenora declared eagerly.

"Remember, we can't be sure it *is* Mike," Beverly cautioned.

"The rider we met said he was tall and dark, with curly black hair and black eyes," Larry said. "That sounds like Mike, doesn't it?"

"In a few minutes we'll know," Mr. Brewster declared. "It should be somewhere on the other side of that rocky slope."

They spurred their horses on, anxious to reach the spot without losing another minute.

They came upon the dead gray ashes of an abandoned campfire. There was evidence that someone had camped here a short time ago, but there was nothing to indicate his identity.

"Well, it may have been Mike," Lenora said slowly, in keen disappointment. "Can't we follow him and make sure?"

"Which way did he go?" Larry asked, shrugging his shoulders. "None of us is a good trail reader."

"It would be hard to follow anyone in this rocky country," Mr. Brewster agreed. He sighed. "We might as well go back to our camp before it is dark. Perhaps tomorrow we'll meet him."

"We've been saying that for days," Lenora complained. "This is the first time we even came close."

They turned about and headed back to their own camp. The return ride was made in gloomy silence, and when they arrived they began silent preparations for their dinner.

"Cheer up, Lenora," Beverly said, smiling, as they sat down to eat. "Mike hasn't disappeared for good. You'll meet him soon—I'm sure of it."

"Think how close we were to that camp and never saw him," Lenora said. "We might pass within a hundred yards of him in the underbrush and still not know it. This country is so big it sometimes scares me."

"We don't have provisions to remain camped here many more days," Larry added a sobering note. "We didn't think it would take this long to locate the gold site—or Mike. We will soon have to return to Red Camp for more supplies."

"I am not leaving until we find him," Lenora said flatly.

"Tomorrow morning Larry and I plan to ride farther through the pass," Mr. Brewster said. "The twin pines must be in that direction."

"There are some beautiful rock formations. You might like to take pictures," Larry suggested to Lenora.

"We'll go with you," Lenora said at once.

Beverly was silent. She had other plans for the morning, but she had to find some way to get away from her friends.

After breakfast the next morning, Larry and Mr. Brewster began to saddle the horses. Beverly remarked that the foot she had caught in the trap was still paining her a little and she thought she would stay in camp to rest it.

"You mean you aren't riding with us this morning?"

Lenora said in surprise. "You'll miss the scenery—and maybe the twin pines."

"I'll see them next time—when we move the camp," Beverly replied, smiling at him.

"I'll stay with you," Larry offered at once.

"No, Larry," Beverly urged. "You go with Mr. Brewster. He may need you. Besides, you can be custodian of Lenora's binoculars and extra film."

"I don't like the idea of you staying here alone," Larry persisted.

"What could happen?" Beverly asked, smiling. "I'm going to rest my foot and read a magazine."

"If Mike rides past, tell him to wait for me," Lenora laughed.

"I'll tell him," Beverly nodded.

She felt guilty about the deception she was practicing upon her friends when they reluctantly rode off without her, but she felt she *had* to talk to Mike without any more delay.

As soon as Larry and the others had disappeared from sight she saddled Lady and rode to where Mike's trailer was parked.

The door of the trailer was closed and Mike did not answer her knock. The car was gone, too. He would not have taken his car to spy again on the little cabin, Beverly thought. He must have gone farther than that. She decided she would try to find him at the old mines. He had said he spent a good deal of his time there.

Lady seemed glad of the exercise as Beverly urged

her to a gallop. She did not want to stay away from camp too long for fear her friends would return and worry about her absence.

She saw the sheepherder they had passed several times before. His dogs were wandering about among the sheep and pricked up their ears when she galloped toward them.

"Good morning!"

Beverly reined in her horse beside that of the weather-tanned herder and responded to his friendly smile.

"Are you lost?" he asked.

"No," she said. "I am looking for the geologist who lives in the trailer back there."

"He passed me about an hour ago," was the response. "He was going out to look at the gold diggings again, I reckon. Funny, isn't it, the fascination gold has for some folks? Me—I've lived around here so long I wouldn't give any mine a second glance. I heard tell, though, that one of the big mining companies back east plans to start digging. They think the gold runs right through the hill."

"I'd like to see some of the old mines," Beverly said, anxious to be on her way. "In which direction do they lie?"

"Since you don't know the country around here, you had better follow the road. You won't miss them." He gestured toward the rising hills. "It used to be an old wagon trail, and it's kind of bumpy for cars, but they manage."

Beverly thanked him and rode off, pausing once to look back and wave. His life must be a lonely one, she thought, but maybe he preferred it that way. The bleating of his sheep died away behind her. Soon she could hear nothing but the pounding of Lady's hoofs on the dusty road.

It was not far to the first deserted mine. There were boards across the entrance to prevent anyone entering the tunnel which led under an overhanging ledge of rock. She went from one to another and soon located Mike's car, but Mike himself was nowhere to be seen.

Beverly dismounted and left Lady by the car. She climbed over the rocks until she stood before the entrance to what looked like a huge cave. On the rock beside the yawning cavity someone had printed in crude letters:

"Danger! Do not enter!"

A broken and discarded shovel, as well as a rusty pick and several bent and battered buckets, attested to the fact that this spot at one time had been the scene of mining activities.

From the proximity of Mike's car she judged he must be somewhere close by. Indeed, there were footprints which could be his leading into the cave opening.

Beverly went back to Lady, drew a small flashlight from the saddlebag, and returned to the cave.

"Hello, in there!"

Her voice echoed along the corridor, but there was no reply.

The narrow white beam from her flashlight swept over the rocky wall and floor. The footprints ended a few feet inside the cave as the dust changed to granite. There was no way of telling how much farther the man who had made the prints had gone. At least, she told herself, he must still be in the cave, because there were no prints leading out.

Beverly went a few steps farther, her light dancing ahead of her. She saw nothing to indicate that anyone else was in the abandoned mine.

Curiosity urged her on, and soon she came to a huge circle of space, like an empty room, with two corridors leading from it. Here the floor was dusty again and there were footprints—so many it was impossible to distinguish those she had seen at the entrance.

When she called aloud her voice resounded hollowly against the rough, jagged walls. There were holes chipped in the walls where hopeful prospectors had tried to obtain ore. There was a cavity in the floor, too, but the digger had tired when he reached a depth of about three feet.

Mike couldn't be here, so there was no use going any farther into the mine.

Beverly turned to make her way out. She had no desire to get lost underground. Then she heard it. There was no doubt it was a human voice.

"Help! Help me! In here!"

CHAPTER XIII

Cave-in

BEVERLY started impulsively toward the tunnel from which the voice had come. It was one of the two leading out from the roomlike space in which she stood.

"Hello!" she called.

"In here! Hurry!"

Suddenly Beverly slowed her steps. She remembered the trap of the old barn and the warnings issued to the girls. Was this another such trap? It would be an ideal place for one.

"Help!" the voice came again, clearer this time.

"Who is it?" Beverly called.

"Please hurry!" the masculine voice implored.

If only she were not alone, Beverly thought desperately. There was no denying the urgency in the voice. But how could she be sure it was no pretense?

"Help!" The voice was desperately pleading now.

"I'm coming!" Beverly called back and plunged ahead.

The corridor was narrow and low. She had to stoop and go cautiously lest she run head on into a jagged piece of rock. Here and there, wooden beams had been propped against the roof of the tunnel in an attempt to keep it from caving in. Beverly regarded her surroundings with misgivings. It certainly was not the safest place in the world to be at the moment.

"Where are you?" she called into the blackness ahead of her.

"Here! Right ahead of you."

The voice was surprisingly close now.

Beverly's little light cut through the darkness, and as she came to an abrupt turn in the tunnel she saw where some of the wooden shoring had fallen under the weight of the rocky ceiling. A man lay caught under a wooden beam.

"Mike!" she cried.

"Is that you, Beverly? I've never been so glad to see anyone!" he declared. "See if you can move this beam. The rocks are resting on the end of it and holding it so that I can't budge."

"Are you hurt?"

Beverly put her weight against the beam at different spots, but at none of them could she move it at all.

"I don't think so," Mike answered. "I'm just caught like a fly on a piece of flypaper. I was looking for an-

A man lay caught under a wooden beam

other entrance to this tunnel when the thing collapsed around my ears."

"It's no use," Beverly said at last. "I can't move it. If only I had something to use as a lever—I know! There is a broken shovel at the entrance. I'll get it."

"Hurry, Bev," Mike implored. "I'm afraid the rest of the ceiling will collapse any minute."

Beverly flung the ray from her flashlight over the roof above them. There was a wide crack and dust was falling from it. There was no doubt the ceiling was settling.

"Save yourself, Bev!" Mike urged. "You can get the others and dig me out later."

"I'll be right back!" Beverly promised.

Without wasting any more time, she darted back along the tunnel to the entrance. For a moment, as she emerged, she was blinded by the brilliant sunlight. She found the broken shovel and also the pick, and turned back immediately into the tunnel without seeing the two horsemen standing silently on the rocks above her.

When Beverly reached Mike, the crack in the ceiling was widening rapidly. It was only a matter of minutes before the roof of the tunnel would collapse, pinning them beneath it.

Mike directed her as she sought to use the handle of the shovel as a lever to move the wooden beam.

"See if you can move that one rock first," Mike urged. "It seems to be holding the rest on the beam."

Beverly worked hastily and silently, a prayer in her

heart. At last the rock rolled free and when she put the handle of the shovel under the wooden beam and bore down with all her might she felt the beam move and a moment later Mike slid free.

"Come on!"

He seized her hand and keeping their heads low, they started to run along the tunnel.

There was a roar behind them and a cloud of dust billowed out and surrounded them. Part of the tunnel had collapsed over the spot where they had been only a moment before! They did not pause to look back, but continued to run until they emerged into the cool, bright sunlight. There they collapsed onto the rocks, gasping for breath.

Beverly was dusty and mussed, while Mike had lost his dark glasses and old hat.

"If anyone saw you now, it wouldn't be hard to penetrate Leahcim's disguise," Beverly declared.

"I'll get back into character as soon as I reach the trailer. If the gold mine belonged to me, Bev, I would give it all to you," Mike said. "If you hadn't come along when you did I would be under the rubble back there."

"And no one would know what had happened to the mysterious young geologist," Beverly said lightly. "Your hand is bleeding."

"It was pinned under a rock," Mike said, flexing his fingers. "Nothing broken. I'm lucky that is all that is wrong."

"I'll ride back to the trailer with you and bandage

your hand for you," Beverly offered. "I want to talk with you."

"Is that how you happened to find me?" Mike asked, smiling. "Is your curiosity bothering you again?"

"Overwhelmingly," she confessed. "How did you know we were in that cabin yesterday?"

"I was watching it," he answered. "I saw you ride up and go inside. I would have remained hidden if the horseman hadn't returned."

"I wonder who he is," Beverly said. "He's been asking for you all over this vicinity. He even went to see old Ben."

"I'm sure he didn't get any satisfaction there," Mike returned. "Where are Larry and Lenora and Mr. Brewster this morning?"

"They are trying to find the twin pines—the rocks near the gold site," Beverly said. "They've gone through the pass."

"Doesn't Mr. Brewster remember the location?" Mike wanted to know.

Beverly shook her head.

"He says he was so ill when you two were here that he was hazy about directions and trusted you implicitly."

Mike sighed deeply.

"I wish he knew I haven't betrayed his trust. But someone else has," he said grimly. "I thought he must be confused about the location of the gold when he didn't take you directly to the spot. Perhaps it is just as well he hasn't found it. You aren't in as much danger as you might have been. The twin pines are visible only after you have gone through the pass and around the base of the cracked fountain."

"What is the cracked fountain?" Beverly asked.

"At one spot water flows from an opening in the rocks," Mike explained. "The formation is such that it gives the impression of a fountain. We found it difficult but not impossible to ride along the ledge of the cliff. If we hadn't, we wouldn't have found the gold. I have a theory that this tunnel runs toward our find—right through the hillside. I believe we could bore through to the gold from this side. I was looking for signs of that when the beam collapsed on me."

"Why don't you come and talk to Mr. Brewster?" Beverly urged. "He will believe you, Mike. I'm sure he will—especially if you take him to the gold now."

"I'll come in a day or two," Mike said grimly, "and I'll have the real thief with me when I do. Wait a minute! I have an idea! If you want to, Bev—" He hesitated. "I don't think the danger would be great."

"What is it, Mike? Is there something I can do?" Beverly asked eagerly.

"I was going to suggest that you lead Mr. Brewster and the others to the gold and I will meet you there," Mike said. "Don't tell them who I am until I come. Then you can tell them your surprise. Tomorrow—yes, by tomorrow I should be ready."

"Ready for what?" Beverly wanted to know.

Mike ignored her question and spoke as if thinking aloud.

"I could reveal myself and they would be sure to follow. I could lead them right into the trap. That's it! Bev, I'll need your help—yours and Larry's, as well as Mr. Brewster's. You can set the trap and I will spring it with the thief. How about it?"

"I'll do anything I can," Beverly agreed.

"Tomorrow, take the others to the gold site and when you get there, try to post them at strategic spots overlooking the gold site. When we arrive you can close in."

"The others are going to wonder how I know about the gold," Beverly declared. "What will I tell them?"

"Nothing," Mike said. "I want to tell the story when the thief is on hand. Your friends will trust you if you ask them to."

"I'll try," Beverly said reluctantly. "It's all awfully vague, Mike."

"It has to be," he insisted. "The thief might not follow the bait, and in that case Mr. Brewster would be disappointed again. Do what I ask, Bev, and trust me to do the rest."

"Very well," Beverly nodded. "Tell me the name of the real thief, Mike."

"You wouldn't know him, Bev, and, besides, tomorrow you will learn everything. Now I've got to do some more spying. We better go back."

Beverly rode Lady and Mike drove his car back to

the trailer. There Beverly bandaged his injured hand and tried to elicit more information from Mike about his plans for the next day, but he refused to explain further.

Mike let Beverly out, and as she walked toward Lady grazing at the edge of the clearing she saw something white move among the trees. Someone had been spying on the trailer! She turned back, but Mike had closed the door. This was her chance to learn more on her own.

She swung into the saddle and urged Lady toward the unknown person moving among the trees. She heard a horse neigh and then hoofbeats, and knew that her quarry had mounted a horse and was fleeing ahead.

Beverly spurred her gentle mount to a swifter pace, dodging the low-hanging branches that swept against her, straining to catch a glimpse of the vanishing figure.

Whoever it was must have seen Beverly leave the trailer and decided there was nothing more important to watch. She wondered if it were the man on the white horse or one of the others who occupied the cabin with him. She could not tell if it were a white horse ahead of her, because the color was not visible through the trees.

The hoofbeats grew fainter and Beverly urged Lady on. Her sure-footed horse galloped eagerly ahead as if she enjoyed the chase. She leaped fallen tree branches, dodged entangling vines, and swerved at the slightest command from her rider.

The spy was not fleeing to the cabin on the hill, and Beverly began to wonder just where the chase would lead her. Perhaps she had not been wise to go in pursuit so impulsively.

Suddenly there was a muffled cry from ahead of her. She reined in her horse and proceeded at a more cautious pace. She came upon a log lying across the path and as Lady halted she saw a figure lying on the ground and a horse grazing docilely near by. It was obvious what had happened: the rider she had been pursuing had been thrown when the horse leaped over the log.

Beverly dismounted and ran to the fallen figure. It was a girl, slender and black-haired, lying face downward. Beverly knelt and gently turned the girl over. As she did so she fell back in surprise. The fallen rider was Betsy Fuller!

CHAPTER XIV

On the Scene

BETSY FULLER—here! Questions crowded into Beverly's mind as she stared at the unconscious girl. What did it mean? How did the girl who had come to their apartment in New York seeking friends and hospitality come to be out here? Why had she been spying on the trailer? Did she know Leahcim was Mike? Was she the girl in the cabin with the man on the white horse?

Beverly looked about at her saddle. She had not brought her canteen of water, but the creek was near by. She laid the girl down gently and ran the fifty yards or so to the narrow creek. She soaked her scarf in the cold mountain water and carried it back to the scene of the accident, then stopped in surprise. Betsy was gone! Her horse had disappeared also. There was no way of telling in which direction she had fled.

Betsy must have been pretending unconsciousness when Beverly found her. And as soon as Beverly moved away she had seized the opportunity to escape.

More puzzled than ever by this latest development, Beverly mounted Lady and rode slowly to the camp she and her friends had established. She began to recall things Betsy had said and done when she was in the girls' apartment. Beverly recalled how Betsy had recognized the picture of the group, including Mike, taken on the *Susabella.* Beverly and Mike were the only ones who had prints of that particular picture. Betsy must have seen Mike's picture. She must have known Mike, but when and where? Why was she out here now? Was she, too, pursuing him?

Beverly no sooner had returned to camp than Lenora and Larry rode in, the latter's horse limping in a forefoot.

"What happened?" Beverly asked.

"Tony seems to have cut his foot," Larry told her, frowning.

"We didn't go as far as we planned to," added Lenora. "We thought we better bring him back to camp."

"Where's Mr. Brewster?" Beverly looked for the fourth member of their party.

"We met old Ben and he stopped to talk with him," Larry explained, examining his horse's foot. "Mr. Brewster thinks Tony will be as good as ever tomorrow. I hope so."

"Then we'll go out again," Lenora said. "The sun might be better for pictures then, too."

"How is your foot, Bev?" Larry asked.

"What? Oh, it's all right," Beverly said hastily.

For a moment she had forgotten the deception she had practiced upon them.

"As a matter of fact, it felt so much better that I took a little ride myself," she said.

"Anything interesting to report?" Lenora inquired. "Every time you go anywhere something happens."

"You will never guess who I saw this morning," Beverly told her, smiling.

"Mike?" Lenora asked eagerly. Then, not waiting for an answer, "That's wishful thinking, of course. Tell us, Bev."

"Betsy Fuller!"

Lenora stared at her for a moment.

"You mean 'Poor Little Me'?"

Lenora's voice was such a close imitation of the way Betsy had spoken in New York that Beverly laughed.

"Is that the girl who came to your apartment in New York?" Larry asked.

Beverly nodded, and described the encounter with Betsy. However, she did not tell them she had followed the girl from the trailer. She could add that when she told them about Mike. She let them think she had only come upon Betsy after the girl had been thrown from her horse. Now it was enough to speculate on why Betsy was here and where she had gone.

"She must be the girl with the man who has the white horse," Lenora guessed. "But why? What is she doing out here? Do you suppose she is looking for Mike, too?"

"Nearly everybody seems to be," Larry laughed. "Didn't she say anything to you girls about making a trip west?"

"No. She told us she had come to New York to get a job and make a career for herself," Beverly replied.

"Shirley said in her letter that Betsy departed without warning," added Lenora.

"The same day we did," finished Beverly.

"Maybe she followed you," Larry offered. "There, Tony," he patted his mount affectionately as he finished bathing the cut foot. "As soon as Mr. Brewster comes, we'll treat it further."

When Mr. Brewster returned to camp the subject changed to Tony's hurt foot and the ride they would take the next morning.

This time Beverly entered enthusiastically into the plans for their search. Without arousing their suspicions, she would have to make sure they took the route Mike wanted them to take and were at the spot where he had planned to spring his trap.

The morning dawned beautifully clear and cool. Tony's foot was very much better, and they were sure he could make the trip.

"We'll go slowly—just in case," Larry said as he saddled his mount.

"All ready?" Lenora was in the saddle with her camera in a case over her shoulder and the binoculars swinging from the saddle horn.

Mr. Brewster led the way, with Beverly following him. He was the one she had to influence as to the direction to be taken, and when the path was wide enough she rode beside him, talking about their objective.

"I seem to recall riding through a pass in the rocks," Mr. Brewster mused as they went along. "After we found the gold we climbed a rocky hillside. There was no established path and it was in clambering over the rocks that I slipped on a loose stone and would have gone crashing down the cliff but for Mike. He saved my life."

"I'm sure he didn't save your life just to rob you later," Beverly said frankly.

Mr. Brewster glanced at her sharply.

"You still insist he is innocent of any wrongdoing?"

"His only wrongdoing was in running away," Beverly said. "I'm sure he didn't rob your desk."

"How can you be so sure of that?" he demanded curtly. "His fingerprints were on it. He didn't touch the drawer in my presence, therefore—"

"Look!" Lenora exclaimed suddenly behind them.

They had been traveling through the mountain pass with rocky walls rising on either side of them. Now, suddenly, they burst out on a low plateau overlooking a narrow, limestone gorge. On their right, gurgling from a crack in the rocky hillside was a trickle of clear, cool water.

The cracked fountain! Beverly recognized it from Mike's description. It was exactly where he said it would be.

"Let's ride around the base of the cliff and see what lies on the other side," Beverly proposed.

"I'd rather go the other way," Lenora protested. "The light is better for pictures—"

Beverly urged Lady to pick her way along the narrow ledge, pretending she hadn't heard Lenora's protest. The others fell in behind her.

Wild, unsettled, beautiful country spread out before them. Entering into it was like entering into another world. Hugging the rocky slope of the hill, their horses made their way along the narrow path. One misstep here could send horse and rider plunging into the depths below. The riders made no attempt to guide their mounts. They let the surefooted little horses pick their own way, instinct guiding them.

At last they rounded the base of the cliff and came out upon a stretch of flat tableland. Rising above them to the east were two stone columns cut by wind and weather to resemble pine trees.

"The twin pines!" Mr. Brewster exclaimed.

"It certainly is rugged country," Larry declared, gazing around him. "How do you ever expect to mine for gold? You would never get heavy mining equipment over the path we followed."

"On the other side of this cliff are several abandoned mines," Mr. Brewster explained. "We expect to utilize them. Mike felt that one or more of them should run almost through the cliff itself, and if that is so, we can take advantage of that fact to pick up where the original miners left off."

"Now that we are here, will you show us the gold vein?" Lenora asked eagerly.

"We might as well look around now that we are here," Beverly agreed, dismounting quickly.

She had to figure out a way to keep them here until Mike arrived.

"Why don't we have our lunch now?" she proposed. "It might be well to rest Tony's foot, too."

The others obligingly agreed to her suggestion, and after they had eaten and the horses were peacefully nibbling at sparse snatches of grass, they walked to the base of the twin pines and Mr. Brewster began looking for marks Mike had said he left at the scene.

There were letters and arrows scratched on the rock, and wooden markers hammered into the ground, all leading to a narrow excavation where Mr. Brewster found a piece of stone showing an unmistakable trace of yellow ore.

"Mike had samples like this assayed and it was found to be of a high grade," he explained. "To the old-time prospectors it must have seemed inaccessible, but today, with modern equipment—"

"I'm going to take a sample," Lenora said eagerly.

"When I get home I want to show my friends what gold looks like in the rough."

"We had better be getting back to our camp," Mr. Brewster remarked. "We don't want to have to negotiate that narrow path in the dark."

"I should say not!" Lenora shivered. "I never expected to make it in the daylight!"

They couldn't leave yet, Beverly thought frantically. Where was Mike? Why didn't he come? They had been here over two hours already and there was no sign of him yet.

"Why don't you take some pictures of the view from here, Lenora?" Beverly suggested. "When Mr. Brewster lets us write the story of the gold mine for the *Tribune* we'll need illustrations."

Lenora looked to the mining man for permission and he nodded.

Another hour went by and still no sign of Mike.

"Is there any other way to get here except by the path we took?" Beverly asked.

"I don't know," Mr. Brewster confessed. "As I told you before, the memory of my previous visit is very confused. There may be."

"I had rather hoped we would find Mike here," Lenora confessed.

"I was sure of it," Larry agreed ruefully. "Shall we be going now?"

"We have a long time before sundown," Beverly said, glancing about desperately.

Where was Mike?

"May I remind you it gets dark quickly out here," Mr. Brewster said. "We better be getting back."

"But I—" Beverly began weakly.

"No one will take Mr. Brewster's gold now," Lenora smiled. "Relax, Bev. We can come back tomorrow."

Tomorrow would not do. Mike had said he would meet them today. Where was he? Should they wait any longer? Mike was depending upon her to have Mr. Brewster and Larry there when he arrived. He wanted to spring his trap on the thief. What would happen if they were not there to help him?

"I wish we could stay a little longer," Beverly murmured.

"For goodness sake, why?" Lenora asked with a little laugh. "I know a lot more comfortable spots."

"How is Tony's foot?" Beverly asked her fiancé, ready to use any excuse for delaying action.

"He doesn't seem to be having any trouble," Larry answered. "What's wrong with you, Bev?"

"Don't you feel well?" Lenora inquired.

"Are you afraid to make the ride along that narrow ledge again?" asked Mr. Brewster.

"Oh, that ride!" Lenora shivered again. "We've got to go, Bev, before it gets dark."

"Wait—" Beverly consulted her wrist watch. "Please wait just a half hour longer. I have my reasons. You'll have to trust me."

"What's up, Bev?" Larry came and took her by the

shoulders. "Tell us what all the mystery is about."

"I can't—yet," Beverly said. "We just have to wait here a little longer. Please, Larry."

Mr. Brewster had been studying her with frowning eyes. Now he left his horse and approached her.

"You have seen Mike, Miss Gray!" he said in a low, tense voice. *"He* told you how to get here—that is why you chose the dangerous path around the cliff instead of going the other way—the way any other stranger would have gone. You knew the gold was here, because Mike told you!"

Beverly was silent. Larry's hands fell from her shoulders and he gazed at her in bewilderment.

"Beverly, is that true?"

"Bev, *have* you seen Mike?" Lenora came to her, too.

Beverly turned away to stare out over the empty stretch of land.

"I can't tell you anything. You must trust me."

"But Mike—is he all right?" Lenora asked anxiously. "Bev, you have to tell us!"

"We trust you, Beverly, but—" Larry began.

"Trust you!" Mr. Brewster exploded. "All these days we've been waiting and searching, and you *knew!* Either you tell me immediately where I can find Mike, or I will have you arrested as an accessory to the theft."

CHAPTER XV

Where Is Mike?

IN THE face of Mr. Brewster's threat Beverly stood firm. She had promised Mike to wait for him and let him make his own explanations. Besides, Mr. Brewster could hardly take any action right at the moment in this forsaken spot. Mike might appear at any moment and then everything would be solved.

"Beverly, you must tell us," Larry pleaded. "Is Mike near by? Was he supposed to meet us here?"

She admitted that much with a nod.

"*Where* is he?" Mr. Brewster demanded. "Is he playing games with us?"

"It is no game to Mike," Beverly defended the young man warmly. "He promised to bring the real thief with him."

"A likely story," Mr. Brewster scoffed.

"I believe you, Bev," Lenora came to her friend's aid. "What did Mike want us to do?"

Beverly smiled gratefully at the blonde girl.

"All I know is that he promised to come here while we were here. He was using himself as bait to lure the real thief to the scene so that Mr. Brewster can learn the truth."

"He hasn't come," Lenora said slowly. "Things couldn't have worked out as he hoped they would."

"The sun will be setting soon," reminded Larry. "What shall we do?"

"It looks as though he isn't coming," Beverly admitted with a sigh. "We might as well return to our camp."

"Perhaps he will send you a message or meet us there," Lenora said hopefully.

They mounted their horses slowly and started toward the narrow ledge over which they must go to reach the cracked fountain and the pass beyond.

"Up there!" Lenora cried suddenly. "I'm sure I saw a man silhouetted against the sky!"

The others turned in the direction she indicated but saw nothing but the jagged gray rocks against the pale blue of the sky.

"Was it Mike?" Larry asked eagerly.

"He was too far away to tell," Lenora replied. "Perhaps we should wait a few minutes longer."

As she spoke they heard a low rumble which grew in intensity until a thundering crash seemed to fill the world, and the very ground under their feet shook.

"A rock slide," Mr. Brewster shouted. "Get close to the wall!"

They urged their quivering horses as close as possible to the protection offered by the cliff side. A shower of small stones and pebbles rattled down around them, and then at last there was only dust and silence.

"If what I think it was happened, we are in trouble," Larry declared. "Wait here."

He rode off in the direction of the ledge over which they had to make their way to leave this small, plateau-like area, and when he returned his face was grim.

"The rocks completely block the path. We are sealed in here," he announced.

"The man Lenora saw—" Mr. Brewster said grimly. "It was a man-made slide."

"It couldn't have been Mike!" Beverly felt urged to speak in the face of his suspicion.

"What are we going to do?" Lenora wanted to know. "Our exit is cut off."

"We'll have to find another one," Beverly said.

Her companions stared at the rocky cliff rising above and around them.

"It would help if we were mountain goats," Lenora attempted a levity she did not feel. "But since we aren't—"

"It is impossible," Mr. Brewster said slowly.

"I saw a man up on the top," Lenora put in. "If he could climb it—"

"He climbed the other side of the cliff," Larry pointed out.

"We'll climb, too," Beverly said. "We can't give up so easily."

"We might do it at that," Larry said slowly. "We'll go zigzag, hunt the easiest footing, and take our time. To the south it seems to rise more gradually."

Mr. Brewster rode up and down along the base of the cliff for quite a distance, and when he halted beside them he did not look as hopeless as he had immediately after the rock slide.

"I think we can make it," he said, dismounting. "It won't be easy or quick, but there must be a way over the top."

Lenora picked up Red's reins.

"Let's start at once. We might be able to go most of the way before it gets dark."

"Not with the horses!" Mr. Brewster exclaimed.

"Certainly with the horses," Beverly said. "We can't abandon them here."

"They will never be able to make the climb."

"You'd be surprised what these sure-footed cow ponies can do," Larry joined in.

"We'll find a path they *can* climb," added Lenora staunchly.

Leading their mounts, they set out to find a place where they could start the ascent of the cliff. Near the twin pines they came upon a ledge of rock jutting upward and outward. They started along it, Mr. Brewster leading the way, coaxing his gray roan behind him. Next came Lenora, urging Red to follow her. Beverly, leading Lady, preceded Larry and Tony. They had misgivings about Tony because of his injured foot, but he started the climb more eagerly than the others.

They made their way slowly but determinedly, back and forth, wherever there was foothold for man and horse, and always upward. When they had stood below and contemplated the cliff there had seemed to be nothing but rock. Now, however, they found openings and hidden trails which could be negotiated with a minimum of difficulty.

Beverly was almost grateful for this situation. Her companions were too worried about their predicament to ask her the questions about Mike which she had expected. She knew she would face a stern cross-examination the minute they arrived safely in their camp, and she did not know how she would answer.

Where *was* Mike? What had happened to him? Who had sent the rocks tumbling down to block their retreat from the gold site?

Suddenly Mr. Brewster called a halt. They had come to a flat table of rock jutting out from the cliff side. The view was beautiful and breathtaking. They stopped to rest and admire the sunset.

"So far it hasn't been as bad as I anticipated," Lenora sighed, "but I'm getting hungry. Let's not linger here."

"I hate to tell you," Mr. Brewster said, "but this seems to be as far as we go."

"What do you mean?"

"Look about you. There are rocks all around us. I don't see any upward path from here, do you?"

Tony nudged Larry's shoulder as they stood contemplating their position.

"He is hungry, too," Lenora observed.

Larry's horse tossed his head and trotted off a few feet, pausing to look over his shoulder at his rider.

"There is a pass between those two rocks over there," Beverly pointed out. "Look—Tony's heading right for it!"

The horse threw up his head and trotted between the rocks, disappearing from sight. They heard his hoofs clattering on and rushed after him.

"He'll get lost!" Lenora cried. "Or we will!"

"He seems to know what he is doing," Larry commented excitedly. "He must have been here before!"

"At this spot?" Lenora asked dryly, hastening to gather up Red's reins. "I thought we were the first Columbuses to be here."

"Remember the man at Double-O Ranch?" Beverly said. "He told us Tony knew this country better than many people."

"If he can lead us out of here, I will personally buy him ten bunches of carrots!" Lenora declared. "Where did he go?"

"Along this way—" Mr. Brewster called them excitedly. "Look—he's waiting for us."

At the top of a rise of ground they saw Tony, his

head high, looking back at them as if he were waiting and longing to be on his way.

"Tony has possibilities we never dreamed of!" Larry chuckled. "What a horse!"

"There goes Lady!" Beverly echoed as her horse trotted off to join the other one.

"When Red decides to join them it won't be without me!" Lenora declared, swinging into the saddle. "Tally-ho, everybody! I'll catch your horses for you."

Mr. Brewster, too, mounted his horse and followed Lenora. Beverly and Larry proceeded on foot. Tony and Lady led the way to the top of the cliff without stopping. Once at the top they stood docilely waiting, breathing hard from the exertion of the last part of the climb.

Lenora and Mr. Brewster gathered up the reins of the leaders, and when Beverly and Larry joined them Lenora indicated the road down.

"This will be easier. Think of it, saved by a couple of horses! Never again will I laugh at an animal's instinct!"

Larry, on Tony's broad back, led the way down the hillside and onto the trail which led to their camp. The moon came up while they rode, flooding the world with brilliant silver light.

"Isn't it romantic?" Lenora sighed, looking at the moon through the treetops. "I could enjoy it if I weren't so worried about Mike. What do you suppose happened to him, Beverly?"

"I wish I knew," Beverly returned.

Mr. Brewster had not spoken a word since they left the hills. He rode the trail wrapped in stony silence, lost in thought. Even Larry's attempts to draw him into conversation met with little response.

As they emerged from a clump of willows they saw a familiar figure coming toward them in the moonlight. It was old Ben on his burro, Charlie.

"Hi, there!" Larry hailed him.

Ben responded with a wave of the hand but did not stop to chat as he usually did.

"That's odd," Lenora commented. "He is usually such a talkative soul."

"He must have had a hard day at the office," Beverly chuckled.

"If he is as hungry as I am, he is probably thinking of the supper he will make himself when he reaches his cabin," added Lenora. "Even a can of beans would taste good to me right now."

A few minutes later they came within sight of their camp. It lay clearly visible in the bright moonlight, and even before they reached it they could see that it was a shambles.

"What's happened?" Lenora gasped. "It looks like a hurricane struck it!"

"A human hurricane," Larry said grimly, pointing to footprints in the dust.

The tents had been slashed, knapsacks emptied on the ground, and provisions scattered about. Their pack horse stood lonely and dejected in the midst of the rubble.

"I'm glad I had my camera with me," Lenora declared. "At least that is in one piece."

"Why?" Beverly asked, indicating the condition of their camp.

"Someone was evidently hunting for something," Larry said grimly. "They didn't overlook a thing!"

CHAPTER XVI

Gone!

BEVERLY had been wondering how she was going to slip away from her friends and go to see Mike. The wrecked condition of their camp provided a good opportunity. While the others set about to bring order out of the chaos, she slipped away, leading Lady until she was safely out of earshot. She knew she should stay and help, but she knew, too, that as soon as everything was in order they would turn to her with questions about Mike. She had to find him and obtain the answers first.

From now on Mr. Brewster would be watching her closely. Either Mike would come back with her to tell his story or she would tell it for him.

The moonlight slipping through the trees painted the underbrush with silver and caused diamonds to dance on the surface of the creek water. Around her was the hushed silence of night in the forest. But Beverly was too worried and preoccupied to notice the beauty of it.

The trailer gleamed in the moonlight. There was no light showing at any of the windows. Everything was quiet. Beverly tied Lady to a tree in the shadows and approached the trailer on foot. She had a premonition of danger. Every instinct told her something was wrong.

Where was Mike? Why hadn't he met them as he had promised? Had something upset his plans? If so, why hadn't he let her know somehow?

She rapped on the trailer door, but there was no answer. She reached up, pulled, and the door opened easily. All was darkness inside.

"Leahcim," she called softly, using that name in case there was someone else with him.

There was no answer.

Beverly ran back to her saddlebag and secured her small flashlight. She returned and directed its sharp white light on the interior of the trailer. She gasped at the wreckage it revealed. Chairs were overturned, and books were scattered about. Cabinets had been emptied on the floor and drawers dumped. The same human hurricane that had hit their camp had evidently swept through the trailer. There was no sign of Mike, but on the floor near the door was a small spot of dried blood.

She felt sure now that when Mike left the trailer it had not been of his own volition. But who had done this? Where had they taken Mike? It looked as though he had played his role of bait for the thief too well. The bait had been taken without springing the trap.

Beverly was bending over examining the blood spot when she became aware that she was not alone. She had heard nothing and seen no one, but she had the feeling that someone was standing behind her looking over her shoulder. She felt a cold chill of fear and wanted to run or scream, but she could not. The person, whoever it was, was between her and the door. She must face him.

Beverly swung her flashlight around and up and almost sobbed in relief as the man blinked in the sudden glare.

"Blood, eh?"

Old Ben, Mike's friend, indicated the spot on the floor.

"Yes," Beverly murmured. "I'm afraid it is Mike's."

Ben looked around as she played her flashlight over the scene in the trailer.

"Must have been quite a fight," he said with satisfaction.

"What do you think happened to Mike?" Beverly asked.

"It's as plain as the nose on your face," he snorted. "He was lookin' for a feller, and a feller was lookin' for him. They musta met here."

"Then what?" Beverly demanded. "Where is Mike *now?*"

"If I knew, I wouldn't be standin' here talkin'!" Ben retorted.

"We've got to find him," Beverly said. "He must be in trouble. He will need help."

"He'll get it," Ben promised. "Give me your light."

He took Beverly's flashlight and stepped outside. He had had years of experience reading trail signs and tracking animals and human beings. Now he applied his knowledge to find out what had happened to his young friend.

Beverly hovered beside him, endeavoring to read what he did in the footprints in the dust.

"Shall I get my friends to help us?" she asked.

"Not yet," Ben grunted. "We can always get 'em when we want 'em."

"The man with the white horse has a cabin up on the hillside," Beverly said. "Do you think Mike went there with him?"

"More than one man came callin' on Mike—by the looks of all these boot tracks," Ben said tersely.

"Were any of the footprints made by a girl?" Beverly wanted to know.

"Were you here?" Ben asked in surprise.

"Not me," Beverly shook her head. "There is a girl with the man on the white horse."

"Hmph!" was Ben's comment and he returned to studying the ground.

"Yep, they took Mike with them," he said positively. "See that mark in the dust? Mike made that to tell me which way he went."

There was a crude, hurriedly drawn circle and a bootprint in the center. Beverly looked at the old man doubtfully.

"He did," Ben insisted. "When he was out here before I taught him to mark his trail that way so if he didn't come back from his gold huntin' I could come and rescue him."

He stood up and pointed up the hillside.

"The bootprint is going that way. That means Mike went that way, too."

"I'll get my friends and we'll go after him," Beverly said at once.

"Not so fast," Ben cautioned. "I want to scout around a little first. I want to find out how many there are of them."

"I'm coming with you," Beverly declared.

Ben shrugged and climbed onto his little gray burro. Beverly mounted Lady and followed the wizened old woodsman as he urged his mount along the trail left by Mike's kidnapers.

An owl hooted dismally from a tree branch overhead. Beverly shivered at the lonely sound. She wondered what her friends were thinking of her absence. It would not be difficult for them to guess where she had gone. If they had seen her leave, Larry would have insisted on accompanying her—and so would

Lenora and Mr. Brewster. At that time she had not wanted company while she talked to Mike. But now—

Ben stopped his burro and dismounted. Beverly did likewise. There was a handkerchief snagged on a bit of dry bush. Ben retrieved it and threw the beam of her flashlight on the initial in the corner.

"It's Mike's," Beverly said.

"There are only two cabins hereabout," Ben muttered.

"The man with the white horse is living in one," Beverly told him.

"The other is an old sheepherder's cabin. Most of the time it's empty," he added and turned to pick up the burro's reins.

This time Ben resumed his journey on foot, leading his donkey. Beverly, mounted on Lady, followed closely. They were silent as shadows moving through the woods. Even the horse and the burro seemed to sense the importance of silence and did not betray their presence in any way.

They smelled wood smoke before they came in view of the small log cabin with smoke curling from its chimney.

"You wait here," Ben directed. "I'm goin' to take a look around."

They tethered their mounts to a tree and Beverly crouched out of sight in the underbrush while the old trapper moved off to circle the cabin.

Not a sound broke the stillness. Those inside the

cabin must be asleep, but where were their horses? Where was Mike?

Time passed and Beverly grew uneasy. If only Larry would miraculously appear on the scene to help. If only Ben would return! Had she been wrong to trust the old man so implicitly? She began to think back over the evening's events.

They had met Ben when they were returning to their camp. When they got to the camp they found it a shambles. Had he done it? Beverly thrust the thought from her. He would have no reason. Certainly he hadn't had anything to do with kidnaping Mike. He was the young man's friend.

Where *was* Ben? Why didn't he return? Had he found another trail and gone off on it without telling her?

Lady whinnied and nuzzled Beverly's sleeve.

"Shsh!" Beverly stroked the horse's neck.

Lady was as tired as her rider and wanted to rest in camp. Beverly had had no idea she would be gone so long when she stole away from her friends.

She determined to take some action herself. Waiting for Ben could go on indefinitely.

She noted how a tall tree cast its shadow across a window of the cabin. By keeping in the shadow, out of the moonlight, she could approach the cabin unseen. A peek in the window would tell her more than Ben could tell from among the trees.

At once she moved away from her horse and stole

slowly toward the cabin. Treading carefully so as not to take a misstep that would make a noise and arouse those inside, she gained the wall of the cabin and leaned against it while she listened tensely. Only the wind in the trees whispered above her.

She sidled up to the window and cautiously peeped in. A fire blazed in the fireplace, but the room was empty. The bunks had not been slept in and the knapsacks lay exactly where she and Lenora had seen them the other day.

The white horse's rider and the others were not here. Evidently, the fire had been left blazing to make smoke and create the impression that the cabin was occupied. She felt that it had been meant to confuse anyone looking for Mike.

Beverly forgot some of her caution and walked to the door. She pushed it open and stood on the threshold of the empty room. Should she call Ben and tell him their suspicions were wrong? That they would have to look for Mike in another place?

The logs in the fireplace fell apart with a shower of sparks, and one of them rolled part way onto the wooden floor. It might easily set the place on fire, and Beverly moved instinctively to push it back. It was sheer carelessness on the part of the cabin's occupants to have left a blazing fire. When they returned they might find the cabin and all their belongings destroyed.

Kneeling on the floor before the fireplace, she heard the door swing shut behind her and knew that her supposition about the cabin being empty had been wrong. Someone must have been standing behind the door when she entered, and now she was trapped.

Slowly Beverly got to her feet.

"I had no idea I would have such an early opportunity to repay your hospitality," a feminine voice said smoothly. "Welcome, Beverly."

CHAPTER XVII

Prisoners

BEVERLY turned around slowly.

Betsy Fuller leaned against the closed door and in her hands she held a rifle.

"You are a long way from Broadway," Beverly commented.

"So are you," Betsy returned.

"Are you on a vacation?" Beverly continued, ignoring the weapon in Betsy's hands.

"Not exactly," Betsy answered. "We were looking for a friend."

"We?" Beverly looked around.

"My brother and a friend of his," Betsy supplied.

At her words something clicked in Beverly's mind. Several pieces of the puzzle fell into place.

"Mr. Brewster said his secretary had gone to Bermuda," Beverly murmured. "Exactly what is your name?"

"Allow me to introduce myself more formally than the last time—Elizabeth Fuller Jones. My nickname is Betsy."

"That explains a lot," Beverly declared.

"I had planned to go to Bermuda," the girl said, "but things didn't work out exactly as we had planned."

"Mike was more clever than you expected," Beverly smiled. "Putting his charts in code thwarted you, didn't it?"

"For a little while," Betsy admitted. "But he had told me about you girls, especially Lenora, and we felt sure he would get in touch with you."

"So you came to us claiming to be a friend of Lois, knowing she wouldn't be there to deny it," Beverly said.

"You wrote the story of Jim's inheritance and their romantic wedding trip, for the *Tribune*," Betsy pointed out shrewdly.

"Was it your brother you met in the station the day we left?" Beverly asked.

"Did you see us?" Betsy exclaimed. "Yes, I met Stephen. He planned this whole thing. We flew out here and stayed in Webster until you arrived in Red Camp."

"You tried to frighten us away by locking Lenora and me in the barn, and you've been watching us to see when we would meet Mike," Beverly concluded.

"That's right," Betsy agreed. "Stephen thought it would be easy to scare you."

For a moment there was silence.

"Well?" Beverly asked.

"Oh, we know who Mike is now," Betsy assured her.

"How did you learn Mike's identity?" Beverly wanted to know.

"Steve and Ralph saw you and Mike leave the mine, and I overheard you with him in the trailer. Steve and Ralph went to see him after I got back."

"Where is Mike now?" Beverly asked.

"He is safe enough," Betsy assured her. "My brother is trying to persuade him to give us a copy of his code."

"Did you think we had the code?" Beverly inquired. "Is that why you wrecked our camp?"

"We felt Mike might have entrusted it to you, since you seemed to be in his confidence."

"When you didn't find it, what did you decide to do?"

"Steve is sure he can get it direct from Mike himself," Betsy assured her.

"I don't think so," Beverly declared. "Mike has gone through too much to give up now. He intends to prove your brother is the real thief."

Betsy shrugged.

"We shall see. Stephen says he can't do that."

"Was it your brother who started the rock slide?"

Beverly asked. "We might all have been killed."

"That was an accident," Betsy answered. "Ralph was watching you, and he slipped and started the slide."

"Stephen is really the brains behind this whole affair, isn't he?" Beverly pursued. "He told you exactly what to do, didn't he?"

Betsy beamed with pride.

"I have a smart brother."

"I don't think he will be smart enough to keep you all out of jail," Beverly commented. "I'll send you a copy of the *Tribune* so you can read about it."

Betsy considered Beverly with startled eyes but said nothing.

Beverly started for the door but Betsy blocked her way.

"My brother told me if anyone came I should keep them here until we are ready to leave," she said.

"Why?" Beverly demanded. "Mike has the code—not I."

"Your being here might prove very useful," Betsy declared.

Oh, fine! Beverly told herself. They would use her as a hostage to threaten Mike. She had to get away!

"I didn't come alone," Beverly said. "You won't be able to keep me here."

"I didn't see anyone with you and I was watching you through the window," Betsy said with a confident smile.

Beverly checked herself. Of course Betsy wouldn't

have seen an experienced woodsman like Ben. He had made sure of that. Beverly's only hope was that Ben had seen her enter the cabin and would somehow rescue her.

Beverly looked about the room. There were two small windows, the door against which Betsy stood, and the door leading into the other room.

"This is the only exit," Betsy assured her, "and I know how to use this rifle."

Beverly made no comment. It might be wiser to wait quietly for Ben to make his first move.

Beverly seated herself on a small wooden bench before the fire. The room was warm and she was tired. With difficulty she stifled a yawn.

She did not believe Stephen Jones and Mike were very far away. She reasoned that Stephen would not want to leave his sister alone very long. They must be in the old deserted sheepherder's cabin. If only she could get out of here!

As it was, Ben might decide to go on seeking his friend and leave her here until he found and freed Mike. Her surprise for Lenora and the others was turning out to be Ben's surprise instead.

Betsy was watching her closely—the way a cat watches the mouse she is planning to devour.

"May I have a drink of water?" Beverly asked.

"There is a thermos jug of spring water over there." Betsy indicated the table across the room. "Help yourself."

"What do you and your brother plan to do when you leave here?" Beverly asked. "You can't get away with it, you know."

"We will," Betsy said confidently. "Steve has a plan."

"Mike will tell the world what you have done," Beverly pointed out.

"We might make Mike a partner," Betsy said. "He could make a fortune. If he refuses—well, I am sure Stephen will think of something."

"You'd be lost without Steve to do your thinking, wouldn't you?" Beverly commented. "I'm sorry for you, Betsy."

"Don't be!" the other girl said airily. "What *are* you doing?"

"I can't get the top off the thermos jug," Beverly replied. "How does it work?"

"Turn it to the right," Betsy directed.

Beverly did as she was told but shook her head.

"It doesn't work."

Betsy moved closer to see what Beverly was doing.

"You're turning it wrong," she said in exasperation. "Turn it to the right."

"I've got it now," Beverly said.

She poured a cup of water and drank it while she considered Betsy thoughtfully. Then she filled the cup a second time and held it out to the other girl.

"Will you have some?"

"No, thanks," Betsy said and moved backward, but it was too late.

The cold spring water splashed directly into her face and in the moment of her confusion Beverly sprang to the door and disappeared outside.

Running like a frightened deer, Beverly at once sought shelter in the dark shadows of the trees. She did not go near her horse, because she could hear Betsy coming after her and she knew the girl would go to Lady first of all.

Beverly crouched low at the base of a protecting tree and listened to the sounds of Betsy thrashing angrily through the underbrush. Once Betsy came within a few feet of Beverly, and the young reporter held her breath until the other girl turned away.

So far so good, but now what? Should she go back to the camp and find Larry? That was quite a distance. She could wait and hide until Ben found her, but that was too indefinite. She could go on and try to find Mike, but what could she do alone?

Above her thoughts Beverly became aware that silence had settled about her. No longer was Betsy thrashing about seeking her. Betsy must have decided to go and warn her brother about Beverly. She would need her brother's advice in a situation like this.

That settled the question in Beverly's mind. The hunted would now become the hunter. She would try to find Betsy and trail her to Stephen and Mike.

First of all, she would send for help. She cautiously made her way to Lady. From her saddlebag she took a notebook and pencil—tools of her profession without which she seldom traveled anywhere. She wrote a few hasty words on a slip of paper and secured it to the saddle. Then she untied Lady and turned her about.

"Go, Lady. Go to camp. Find Tony. Get help!"

Lady trotted a few feet and stopped. She glanced back at Beverly.

"Help, Lady. Get help!" urged Beverly in a whisper. "Go to camp."

The little horse pawed the ground and tossed her head uncertainly. Then she set off at a trot down the narrow trail without another backward glance.

"I hope she is as smart as she is supposed to be," Beverly thought fervently.

If Lady succeeded in reaching camp, help would soon be on the way. In the meantime she had work to do. She patted Ben's burro which was still tethered where the woodsman had left him, and started out. Ben had indicated that the sheepherder's cabin lay to the north and Beverly turned in that direction, carefully dropping a trail of shredded notebook paper behind her as she moved.

The moonlight clearly revealed the only path leading northward through the trees. Beverly started along it cautiously. Betsy was somewhere ahead of her—with the rifle in her hands. From time to time Beverly stopped to listen for sounds of the other girl, but there were none. Betsy had regained her composure and was traveling more discreetly.

With nothing to guide her, Beverly began to wonder

if she were proceeding in the right direction. Perhaps she had been mistaken in her surmise that it was in the sheepherder's cabin that Mike was held prisoner. She wished she had asked Ben how far away it was. And where was Ben? She felt she should have had some sign of him in all this time.

Beverly paused to listen and get her bearings. The trail was almost obliterated at this point. Underbrush and scraggy young trees were thick on all sides. The trail could not have been used much in the past year. It was a perfect hiding place.

As she started forward again, a misstep sent a shower of pebbles cascading down the path. The noise echoed loudly and clearly against the hillside. With her heart beating fast, Beverly apprehensively crouched and waited for discovery. When nothing happened she moved on cautiously. That should tell anyone ahead of her that she was coming, she thought despairingly.

What had happened to Betsy? Was she so familiar with the countryside that she had gone swiftly and unerringly to the other cabin before Beverly could over-take her?

"All right now, put your hands up and turn around!"

The voice broke the silence like a pistol shot and Beverly swung about to obey the command. There was no one behind her. Then she heard a noise off to the right, about fifty yards away. Making herself as small and inconspicuous as possible, she crept over to see what was happening.

Ben stood with his hands in the air. Another man, young and fiercely determined, was pointing a revolver at the old woodsman.

Beverly looked searchingly around and then she saw it. The drab, weather-beaten look provided good camouflage for the little cabin. It was almost lost in the surrounding darkness.

Fumbling about at her feet, Beverly found a rock and tossed it as far as she could. It fell through the tree branches with a loud, crashing noise.

Ben's captor whirled about and his gun accidentally went off. The shot echoed through the hills and brought another man running from the cabin.

"Ralph! What is it? Who's that you have there?"

The two men were so excited over the shot and their captive that they failed to notice the slender figure that emerged from the woods and slipped through the open door of the cabin.

"Beverly! What are you doing here? Get out while you can!"

Beverly paused in the shelter of the door and looked around the barren, dusty room. A smoky, flickering kerosene lamp on the table provided the only illumination. At one place the roof sagged dangerously, and the fireplace had begun to crumble. It was beside these fallen stones that Mike lay, his hands bound behind him.

"Are you all right, Mike?"

Beverly ran to him and set to work on his bonds.

Beverly ran to him and set to work on his bonds

"I'm cold and hungry," he grunted, "but otherwise all right. Leave here at once, Bev. You should never have come in. These men are mad for gold and desperate. They will be back in a moment."

"I can't get this knot loose," Beverly muttered depairingly.

"Too late now!" Mike groaned as the voices outside grew louder.

Bevery looked about for a place to hide. The only spot large enough to shelter her was behind the stones from the fireplace.

"The rifle—" Mike whispered. "Get it quickly!"

Beverly seized the rifle which had been leaning against the wall inside the door, and hurried to secrete herself as Ben was pushed into the room.

"You can join your friend over there. Maybe you can persuade him that it would be better for both of you if he told us exactly how to find the gold."

The man Beverly and Lenora had seen in the restaurant in Red Camp, and whom Beverly had seen at the trailer, pushed old Ben roughly before him.

The second man, the one Beverly and Lenora had seen meet Betsy in the New York railroad station, closed the door behind them and glanced out the window.

"I don't like it, Steve. There is someone else out there in the woods."

"It was probably a squirrel you heard," Betsy's brother replied.

"I don't like it," the first man repeated. "You and your sister talked me into joining you to look for gold, not for kidnaping."

"By tomorrow we'll have the gold and no one will know what we did to get the charts," Stephen Jones said ruthlessly.

"What was that?" The dark-haired man jumped nervously. "I heard something outside."

"Don't be so jumpy—" began Steve.

The cabin door opened and Betsy, disheveled and white-faced in the lamplight, stumbled breathlessly into the room.

"I'd have been here sooner, but I lost the path," she said. "Steve, we've got to get out of here. Beverly will bring the sheriff, I know she will!"

"That won't be for hours," Steve said after his sister gave him a brief account of what had happened in the other cabin. "We can take these two to a cave I found up on the hillside. No one will ever find us there."

"We better give up this whole idea," Betsy said. "Let's leave them here and get away while we can."

"I'm in favor of that," Ralph declared.

"No!" Betsy's brother exploded. "We've risked everything to come this far, and now when the gold is right under our noses you want to run away. I won't do it. With the information about this gold deposit in my possession, the Jones Mining Company can really get started. Changing the names on the papers is simple, but we need Mike's code to interpret the charts. I mean to have that gold—somehow!"

"Steve," the second man said slowly, "where is your rifle? You left it standing by the door—"

Steve and Betsy exchanged startled glances.

"I have it and I know how to use it," Beverly announced, revealing herself suddenly and dramatically, the rifle pointed at the three lawbreakers.

Ben rose, smiling broadly, from where he had crouched beside Mike. The latter, too, stood up and Ben managed to untie his hands.

"Nice work, Beverly," Mike declared, seizing Steve's revolver while Ben took the rifle from Betsy. "We'll take them down to my trailer and send for the sheriff."

But Stephen Jones was not to be defeated so easily. A swift kick sent the table crashing over, smashing the lamp and plunging the cabin into darkness.

CHAPTER XVIII

Captured

THE flickering campfire deepened the shadows on the faces of the three anxious people gathered around it.

"Why didn't she tell us where she was going?" Lenora repeated over and over.

"It is obvious she went to meet Mike," Mr. Brewster declared angrily. "I don't like it. I don't like it at all!"

Some semblance of order had been restored to the camp, although it would never be the same as when they had originally set it up. In the midst of their work they had missed Beverly. It did not take long to determine that Lady, too, was missing, and ever since they had worried and waited.

They tried to eat a cold, improvised meal, but no one had any appetite.

"I'm going after her," Larry said, getting to his feet.

"Where will you start? We don't know which way she went," Lenora pointed out.

"That's true," Larry admitted, "but I think I'll look up that fellow, Leahcim. Beverly has been acting strangely ever since her talk with him the other day."

"Maybe he told her something about Mike!" Lenora exclaimed. "Larry, I'm coming with you."

"We'll all go," Mr. Brewster added.

"What if Beverly returns while we are gone?" Lenora asked.

"We'll leave a note and tell her where we have gone," Larry decided.

"It isn't like Beverly to be so secretive," Lenora complained as they went to get their horses. "I wish she had told me more about Mike."

"We all wish that," Mr. Brewster said grimly. "It is beginning to look as though Miss Gray herself is involved in this thing."

"Beverly had nothing to do with the theft!" Larry denied swiftly.

"She seems to be shielding the criminal," Mr. Brewster returned. He sighed. "I never thought my friendship with Mike would end like this."

"If Mike came to you now and told you he is innocent, would you believe him?" Lenora asked.

"In the face of the evidence against him?" Mr. Brewster shook his head. "I don't know. How could he explain it?"

"Beverly must be trying to help prove his innocence," Larry said, "and she must be in trouble. I can think of no other explanation for her actions."

"Let's try to find her," Lenora urged.

They mounted their weary horses and set out, following the creek downstream until they came in sight of the trailer.

"It's all dark," Lenora commented as they halted in the clearing. "Leahcim can't be at home."

"I'll make sure," Larry said.

The young man took a flashlight from his saddle-bag and approached the trailer. The door was open and he stepped inside. When he reappeared a moment later he ran excitedly to his companions.

"The place is in a mess," he reported. "Something is going on and Beverly must be in the middle of it. What will we do—"

"Shsh!" Lenora held up her hand. "I thought I heard hoofbeats."

They sat perfectly still, listening. At first faintly, and then ever nearer, they heard the clattering of a horse's hoofs descending the hillside.

"Let's go meet the rider," Lenora proposed. "It might be Beverly."

They wheeled their mounts about and three abreast they rode toward the sound of the other horse.

A brown-and-white pony, riderless, burst from the forest in front of them. Startled, she drew back and disappeared among the trees.

"It's Lady!" Larry shouted. "Catch her!"

The little pony took to her heels, racing ahead of them with the elusiveness of a ghost. They fanned out and galloped ahead until they had her between them. Then Lady stopped and stood still, her head hanging dejectedly until Larry was almost close enough to seize her bridle. Suddenly she darted away again. They took up the chase again, until at last Mr. Brewster succeeded in throwing a rope over her head.

"I wonder if she threw Beverly and left her lying somewhere in the darkness?" Lenora said fearfully.

"Wait!" Larry exclaimed. "There is a note on the saddle."

A flashlight was brought to shine upon Beverly's hastily scrawled message. Larry read it aloud:

" 'Am on Mike's trail. Come to cabin Lenora knows. Follow trail of torn paper. Hurry!' "

"Lenora!" Larry swung upon the blonde girl. "Can you lead the way to that cabin?"

"Follow me!" Lenora urged Red into action.

The three riders galloped up the hillside with Lady following. Once Lenora took a wrong trail but corrected her direction with the loss of only a few minutes.

They reached the cabin and saw no one. Dismounting, they began to search for Beverly's trail. They came upon Ben's burro and their mystification deepened.

"Here it is!" Lenora cried. "Lady must have been tied close to the burro. Look at the paper on the ground!"

"It leads this way," added Larry.

They started up the hillside, moving slowly. Some of the scraps of paper had been disturbed by the breeze and scattered about, but there was enough to guide them along the trail Beverly had taken.

"What was that?" Mr. Brewster held up his hand to call a halt.

"It sounded like a shot!" Larry muttered fearfully. "I hope we aren't too late."

They started forward again with renewed vigor, realizing that somewhere up ahead of them a desperate drama was being played.

"It will give me great personal satisfaction to be on the scene for the climax of this hunt," Mr. Brewster murmured.

"I wish we knew what was going on," Lenora said anxiously.

"That's a cabin up there," Larry exclaimed, motioning his friends to halt. "I wish—"

Without warning a crash sounded in the cabin and a moment later the door was flung open. Two men and a girl fled out into the night, with two more men and another girl pursuing them.

"It's Beverly!" Larry shouted. "Bev! Here we are!"

Beverly turned about as her companions continued in pursuit of the three running figures.

"Catch them, Larry!" Beverly cried. "They are the ones who robbed Mr. Brewster!"

Larry and Mr. Brewster raced after them.

The three fugitives ran into the protecting blackness of the trees. Once there, they separated and each endeavored to hide himself as best he could.

Mike, Ben, Larry, and Mr. Brewster relentlessly followed, determined to capture them.

"Lenora, I have an idea," Beverly said. "Come along with me."

"Where are we going? And what are you going to do with that?" Lenora indicated the rifle Beverly still carried.

"Maybe I can capture three desperate people with it," Beverly replied grimly. "I have an idea that girl, especially, won't run very far through the woods. Suppose we sit down and wait for her."

"I like the 'sit down' part," Lenora confessed. "This has certainly been a long day and a busy one! Tell me, Bev, was one of those men Mike?"

"It was," Beverly said, smiling. "He'll tell you his story as soon as Betsy and her brother and their friend are captured."

"Betsy!" Lenora exclaimed increduously.

Beverly nodded. " 'Poor-Little-Me' in person," she said. "She's in this business up to her eyebrows."

The girls reached the cabin where Betsy and her brother had been living. A glance inside told them it was empty.

"Now what?" Lenora asked.

"We are going to wait for them," Beverly said. "We'll hide among the trees where we can watch the door.

I am sure she will come. If she does, her brother will, too."

"And the other man?"

"He is the unknown quantity," Beverly replied. "It is hard to say what he will do."

The girls took up their stand in the shadows. Their horses were across the clearing, chafing impatiently to be on their way back to camp.

"I hope the horses don't scare our quarry," Lenora whispered. "If they hear them they may be afraid to approach the cabin."

"Everything they have with them on the trip is in there," Beverly said. "Even if they only intend to hide in a cave, they will need food, water, ammunition—"

"I see what you mean," Lenora nodded. "The cabin is the mousetrap that will—"

Beverly's hand on her arm silenced her. A slender figure had slipped from the trees and was running swiftly toward the cabin. Betsy gained the shelter of the door and slipped inside.

"Well?" Lenora urged as her friend did not move.

"Wait," Beverly counseled.

Several seconds passed and then another figure, a man, slid furtively out of the shadows and raced to the cabin.

"Your hunch was right!" Lenora whispered delightedly. "What about number three?"

"I'll wait a few more minutes," Beverly said. "You go and get Larry and Mike."

Lenora departed noiselessly and hastily while Beverly kept her eyes on the cabin door.

After what Ralph had said in the little cabin, Beverly felt that he was concerned mostly in saving himself now, and she had little hope that he would join his partners. He was probably as far away as possible.

The cabin door opened and Betsy and Stephen Jones slipped out. They glanced furtively around and then began to move toward the horses they could hear among the trees.

"Stop! Stay where you are!"

Beverly revealed herself, the rifle poised and ready.

"Go back into the cabin," she ordered.

Betsy turned immediately, but her brother stopped her.

"Don't listen to her, Betsy. We'll leave here on their horses. We can be miles away by morning. We will head for the Canadian border."

"But, Steve—" Betsy looked close to tears. "I had no idea where it would all lead when I first agreed to your scheme. Perhaps if you gave back all the charts and papers—"

"Don't be foolish," her brother commanded. "We're leaving."

"Don't move," Beverly ordered. "Go back into the cabin."

All at once a smirk appeared on the face of Stephen Jones, and Beverly felt a presence behind her. In dismay she realized that the third man had not fled as she had taken for granted. He was here now and he was a threat to her. She wanted to turn around and face him, but she was afraid to take her eyes off Steve.

"Beverly, look out!" Betsy screamed.

At the same moment something swished through the air. Beverly leaped aside and the loop of a rope brushed her arm as the man behind her sought to lasso her.

In the same moment Larry and Mike burst from the trail and came running toward the cabin.

CHAPTER XIX

Plans

"I NEVER dreamed it was you," Lenora declared, shaking her head. "That awful red hair!"

"I told you that first day you met me," Mike said, chuckling at the surprise on her face. "I said, 'I'm Leahcim.'"

"I don't usually go around spelling people's names backwards," Lenora protested. "I didn't realize it was Michael."

"Dying your hair certainly changed your appearance," Larry commented.

"Not enough," Mike said ruefully. "Miss Jones and her brother recognized me."

"I don't believe they became suspicious until they saw you with me," Beverly put in.

The excitement was over. The group was back in Red Camp having a leisurely meal in the Gold Nugget. Betsy, her brother Steve, and Ralph had been brought to the sheriff's office; the stolen papers had been found in Steve's knapsack; Mike had told Mr. Brewster the true story of what had happened, and the way was now clear for the Brewster Mining Company to begin operations.

"I never suspected Miss Jones," Mr. Brewster sadly shook his head. "As my secretary, it was easy for her to get the details of my work. But I trusted her."

"Betsy, or Miss Jones, is truly sorry for what she did," Beverly declared. "She told me she wished she had never agreed to do as Steve asked. She's been completely under her brother's influence all her life, and he led her to believe that the gold would be easy to get."

"What do you think will happen to her?" Lenora asked. "She didn't do the actual stealing—"

"She was an accessory," Mr. Brewster replied with a frown. "She might escape jail if she can prove it was her brother's domination that led her into the situation, and ask for clemency."

"Now you can tell us where you kept the code that Steve tried so hard to get," Beverly said to Mike.

"In my memory," he grinned. "I didn't put it in writing for anyone to steal."

"It was a long way to come for a story for the *Tribune,* but it was worth it." Beverly said. Then she sighed. "Well, now I suppose it's back to New York and the office."

"There is one thing I must do first," Lenora said.

"I promised Larry's horse Tony ten bunches of carrots the day he led us out of the rocks, and carrots he shall have! I am going to buy all the general store has. Then I'll board that bumpety bus back to Colber with you."

"That, at least, you shall be spared," Mike declared.

"How's that?" Larry inquired. "We have to go to Colber to take the train."

"We certainly do," Lenora giggled. "Fond as I am of Red, I do not intend to ride a horse all the way to New York!"

"I wouldn't put it past you," Mike laughed, giving Lenora a look of obvious admiration. "But all I meant was that I'll drive you all over to Colber in the trailer."

"Wonderful!" Beverly exclaimed. "But how about you, Mike?"

"I'll have to return the trailer to a friend who loaned it to me," Mike explained, "and then I'll get a train to New York from there. Mr. Brewster," he added, grinning at the older man, "says I'm still working for him."

"You certainly are, young man," John Brewster declared. "And one of these days we'll discuss the idea of your coming in as a junior partner."

"Mike!" Lenora almost squealed in her excitement. "How simply terrific!"

So it was on a happy note the next morning that the four long-time friends and Mr. Brewster began their cross-country journey back to New York, where still more excitement and adventures awaited them.